MELT WITH YOU

Into The Fire Series

J.H. CROIX

ISBN: 9781729140222

Cover design by Cormar Covers

Cover Photography: Eric Battershell

Cover model: Mike Chabot

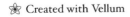 Created with Vellum

"You have to keep breaking your heart until it opens." -Rumi

Sign up for my newsletter for information on new releases & get a FREE copy of one of my books!

http://jhcroixauthor.com/subscribe/

Follow me!
jhcroix@jhcroix.com
https://amazon.com/author/jhcroix
https://www.bookbub.com/authors/j-h-croix
https://www.facebook.com/jhcroix

MELT WITH YOU

Harlow

A wedding, a one-night stand, and no happily-ever-after.

That's how it all started with Max Channing.

Along comes another cliché – a second chance.

A year later, I'm about to face Christmas alone when tall, dark & s*xy as h*ll Max shows up again.

Our lives are worlds apart. He's a billionaire tech investor.

I'm a hotshot firefighter.

Nothing about us makes any sense.

I never thought I'd see him again after the hottest night of my life.

I was wrong, so very wrong.

When our paths cross again, we break every rule.

And set each other on fire.

Max

Harlow May tests every limit I have and makes me want to break every d*mn rule she creates.

She's a temptation I can't seem to resist.

She fits no category. She's strong & sassy and a firefighter
to boot.
She fights the fire between us.
Once I have a taste, no one else will do.
I'll fight for her and for us.
I only want one woman. Harlow.

*This is a full-length, standalone romance with a guaranteed
HEA.

Chapter One

MAX

Somehow, while attending a wedding almost in the middle-of-nowhere Alaska, I'd ended up handling taxi duties. Go figure. According to the latest update sent to me via frantic text from the bride, there was only one straggler left. Within minutes, I was rolling to a stop in front of the hotel, and my phone buzzed in my pocket. Sliding it out, I glanced down.

Harlow May is her name. Find her!

This text came from Ivy Nash—the bride, and the woman Owen Manning had fallen so hard and fast for, I was still questioning his sanity. Ivy was perfect for Owen. I considered teasing her and telling her Harlow was gone. But no. It was Ivy's day, so I'd behave.

On it. She'll be delivered to the wedding shortly.

I'd expected this last guest, who seemed quite important to Ivy, to be waiting outside. Not so. Harlow May was late.

I thought I'd recognized Harlow's name. She was the daughter of an investor for Owen's company, and I happened to be familiar with her father through business connections. Owen and I had met at MIT some years back, and he'd remained one of my closest friends. Off the Grid was his baby, his world-class multimillion-dollar engineering firm, situated in the middle-of-fucking-nowhere Alaska.

After another few beats of waiting, I strolled into the lobby. The wedding was taking place on top of a mountain, at Last Frontier Lodge. Since the wilderness resort was booked out so far in advance, there wasn't enough room there for all the wedding guests, so this hotel served as over-flow. Just as I was about to go to the desk and ask for Harlow to be called, a woman came hurrying out of the elevators.

Inside of a millisecond, I was completely distracted, enchanted, and then some. She had straight, glossy brown hair that hung almost to her waist, and dark brown eyes. Aside from the fact she was flat-out beautiful, she wore a cream silk dress, the outfit as out of place as a giraffe in the midst of a room full of dogs, what with most of the guests around here dressed for the outdoors.

I watched as she hurried through the front entrance, then followed after her. My stride closed the distance between us, my eyes locked on the swing of her hips. She had curves for days, filling out the silk dress. The material swung just above her knees in a ruffle, hugged her hips like a lover, and dipped in at her waist, only to flare out again to cup her breasts.

Stepping through the doors, I walked directly to her, my body tightening the moment I reached her. "Harlow May?"

Her espresso gaze swung to mine. "Yes. Are you the driver?"

I bit back a laugh. "I presume you're attending Owen and Ivy's wedding?"

Harlow twirled a long lock around her finger, and the motion made me want to tangle a hand in her hair and muss it. I didn't, though it took an act of will. At her nod, I gestured to the car. It wasn't my vehicle, it was Owen's decked-out black SUV, with every tech feature you could imagine, and entirely electric. It felt as if I were temporarily living a borrowed life.

"Am I late?" Harlow asked as she stepped over to the SUV.

Her scent drifted up to me, a hint of honey and vanilla. "I don't know if you're late, but you're the last one," I said. She'd missed the first three scheduled trips, but I no longer cared.

I opened the door for her, glancing down to see a flush crest on her cheeks. She slipped into the front seat and buckled her seatbelt. Once we were en route to the lodge, my eyes flicked sideways, landing on the curve of her thigh. My hand itched to slide over the silk, to feel the heat of her skin penetrating through it. I didn't know what it was about her, but I hadn't been this curious about a woman in, well, longer than I could remember.

"So, Harlow, how do you know the bride and groom?"

I thought I knew the answer to my question, but I figured I'd ask anyway.

"I met Ivy and Owen through my father because he's an investor in their company. I'm here for the wedding because Ivy's become a friend. Alaska was on my bucket list too."

"Alaska is quite beautiful, definitely bucket list-worthy."

I rolled to a stop at an intersection, glancing over to find Harlow's gaze on me. "I don't think I caught your name," she said.

She crossed and uncrossed her legs, tempting me to touch her again. Forcing my gaze forward, I turned onto the road that wound up into the mountains.

"Max. Max Channing," I replied.

"Are you just a driver, or here for the wedding?"

"I'm a friend, and driving as a favor," I replied.

I didn't know why, but I preferred Harlow didn't know how our worlds might intersect. Within minutes, we were pulling up in front of Last Frontier Lodge, the spectacular setting for Owen and Ivy's wedding. Diamond Creek, Alaska was one of Alaska's coastal jewels, with the mountains dipping their toes in the sea here.

As I opened the door for Harlow to step out, I caught a glimpse of blue silk between her thighs. I was a gentleman, and wasn't prone to trying to catch sneak shots of women's panties. But sweet hell, Harlow was a magnet for me, and my eyes had a will of their own.

Of all the factors I had considered in coming to this wedding, encountering a woman so delectable I could hardly keep my body in check wasn't on the list. Not to mention, I wasn't on the best terms with her father. In fact, the last time we'd crossed paths, I'd told him he was a fucking asshole. Because he was.

As I walked behind her up the entrance stairs, I idly wondered what she did, but now wasn't the time for chitchat. We only had a half an hour before the wedding started. As we strolled through the door, I rested my hand on her back, guiding her inside and savoring the heat of the silk against her skin.

If Harlow noticed my touch, she didn't react. We walked through the crowded lobby and restaurant, and onto the back deck. Guests were milling about, yet Owen and Ivy were nowhere in sight. I glanced down to Harlow. "Seating's over there. Check with Delia," I said, gesturing to a woman who ran the restaurant at the lodge and was also a wedding guest.

When Harlow glanced at me, I noticed how her dark lashes curled against her cheeks. I couldn't have looked away if I tried as a slow smile stretched across her face, and I had a sudden urge to kiss her.

"Actually, I'm a bridesmaid. Thank you for the ride," she said softly before turning away. She paused beside Delia, her dark hair a contrast to Delia's honey blonde. They briefly conferred, and then Harlow slipped through a side door back into the lodge.

As much as I wanted to linger, I had duties to attend to. I walked back into the lodge to hunt down Owen and found him, with Derek Bridges, in one of the rooms set aside for dressing. Along with Owen, Derek was one of my closest friends from our days at MIT.

Owen was leaning against the dresser, ready in his suit and tie, while he laughed at something Derek said. He glanced my way. "Did you round up everybody?"

"Of course I did. Just ferried the last guest. Harlow May. She's Howard May's daughter, right?"

Owen nodded, his blue eyes crinkling at the corners as he grinned. "Yes. Harlow and Ivy are close."

Derek stood from where he was seated by the windows. "Aren't we all relieved Howard couldn't make it to the wedding?" he asked with a wry grin.

"I gather his daughter is nicer than he is if she's one of Ivy's bridesmaids," I replied.

Owen chuckled. "Ivy adores her, and she's nothing like her father. In fact, he's cranky because she's refusing to work for him."

Just as I was about to counter with a question—because I was *that* curious about Harlow—there was a knock at the door, and Garrett Hamilton poked his head inside, flashing a grin when he saw us. "I've been ordered to come fetch you boys."

In the short time I'd been here, I'd met the Hamilton family in a whirlwind. They owned this ski resort, which was primarily run by the eldest brother, Gage. Garrett was a former corporate lawyer who still practiced law, but he'd said goodbye to his high-flying career in Seattle and moved up here to marry Delia.

Glancing at Owen, I asked, "You ready for this?"

Owen, with his jet-black hair, ice blue eyes, and calm demeanor, actually looked a tad apprehensive. His shoulders rose and fell with a breath as he pushed away from the dresser. Adjusting his tie, he met me at the door with Derek behind him. "Ready as I'll ever be."

Garrett had already started to walk down the hallway. "Let's do this," Derek added, clapping Owen on the shoulder. "Now would be the time to speak up if you have any doubts."

We had started to file out when Owen came to a complete stop, turning back to face us. "I have no doubts. If you're wondering, I'm half-terrified Ivy might suddenly come to her senses. If she does, I don't know what I'll do," he said flatly.

His eyes met mine, the depth of emotion contained there almost startling. "I don't think you need to worry about that," I heard myself saying.

Barely a hint of relief entered his gaze as he turned around.

We filed down the hall and onto the back deck of the lodge, which had been transformed into an outdoor wedding chapel. As I took my place beside Derek at the front, I contemplated how Owen had once been just as unlikely as me to settle down. Yet, here he was, head over heels in love with Ivy.

He had his reasons for keeping to himself, as did I. I still couldn't quite imagine caring that deeply for someone. I'd all but written the idea of love out of my life. As the pastor began the ceremony, I scanned the crowd. My eyes made their way to Harlow, who stood with two other women beside Ivy. The moment I saw her, lust washed over me. I could most certainly imagine a night between the sheets with Harlow.

I couldn't quite get a bead on her. She was quiet and gave off an air of steely strength. I wanted to know more.

Forcing my gaze from her, I took a moment to scan the horizon. Mountain peaks rose all around us, and Kachemak Bay was visible in the distance, the sun striking sparks on its surface. On the heels of a breath, savoring the crisp and cool mountain air, I turned back and watched one of my closest friends get married.

I wasn't usually one for weddings. Yet, this wasn't a typical wedding—outdoors, on the back deck of a beautiful lodge, with the mountains and the ocean serving as the cathedral for the ceremony. My eyes were again drawn to Harlow, as if she were my own personal magnet.

With a forceful mental shake, I tore my gaze free. Relationships were another part of business for me; a way to meet my needs, and nothing more. Love—the flash in the pan, crazy love that Owen had stumbled into with Ivy—well, that wasn't for me.

Chapter Two

HARLOW

After the wedding ceremony, the sky started to cloud, and the guests were herded inside. The lodge was busy, even though it was only autumn. They catered to tourists for every season. I leaned against the bar, sipping my pomegranate martini. I didn't drink often, but I did enjoy a good martini. I was working on my third at this point, but I figured, what the hell? I was at a wedding for one of my dearest friends, happy to escape the pressures of my life.

When Ivy had asked me to be one of her bridesmaids, my only hesitation had been whether or not my father was coming. Ivy, being the friend she was, had been sympathetic but still begged me to come. She'd also gleefully called me when my father bowed out. Owen had invited him, merely out of courtesy, since he invested quite generously in their company.

"Hey, hey," Ivy's voice called.

Spinning around, I leaned my hips against the barstool and smiled.

"Are you glad you came?" she asked when she reached me.

She was glowing, in her cream silk dress, with her amber hair and eyes. I was so happy for her. She and Owen were perfect for each other, the kind of perfect that didn't come along very often.

"Of course I'm happy I came. I think I might stay a little longer than I planned. When do you leave for your honeymoon?" I asked.

Ivy leaned against the bar beside me, glancing over her shoulder to catch the eye of Gage Hamilton. He was the owner of the lodge and had been taking turns bartending with his brother, Garrett. He was quite handsome with his gray eyes and dark hair. He was also quite taken. Not that I felt any kind of spark with him, not at all.

"Give me what she's having," Ivy said to Gage.

He flashed a smile and mixed her drink while he carried on a conversation with another customer.

"We're leaving tomorrow," Ivy replied. "I wish you would stay longer."

"Why? You won't be here."

"Because it makes me happy to think you can have some downtime. You can stay at the house if you'd like. I know how you feel about hotels."

I hated them. Well, hate wasn't the word; they just felt so impersonal. Much of my childhood had been spent in hotels. My mother died when I was young, and work was all that mattered to my father. He traveled a lot and carted me around with him, rotating through babysitters as needed.

I glanced at her as she took her drink from Gage. "Really? That makes the idea more tempting."

"Of course. We'll be gone for two weeks. The house is all yours. You can stay there when we get back too."

I cast a smile her way and shook my head. "I might take you up on staying while y'all are gone, but I'm not crowding your house right after your honeymoon."

Ivy shrugged. "We've been living together for years. My God, it's almost embarrassing it took us this long to get around to the wedding. Why don't you just move out here anyway? You're always saying you want a change of pace."

Home, as it was at the moment, was coastal North Carolina, where my mother was originally from, and where my father's company had its base. Lately, I had found it smothering because all my father wanted was for me to join his company, and I refused. In fact, over the last year or more, I'd done the craziest thing ever. Or not, depending on how you looked at it. My father certainly thought it was ridiculous for me to train to become a hotshot firefighter.

It was quite tempting to pull up stakes and move to Alaska. I would have a built-in best friend and settle into a life far from my father. Even though Ivy and I had only met over the past year, we'd bonded quickly. That was saying something for me because, with all the travel when I was little, I hadn't had many opportunities to make friends. Ivy and I met at a function for the company she shared with Owen and connected instantly.

Catching her eyes, I shrugged. "We'll see. Meanwhile, tell me about Max."

Max, the driver who'd picked me up at the hotel, sent heat sliding through my veins and my belly spinning in flips. Max was *way* too handsome for his own good, and I was *way* too curious for mine.

Even if it didn't make a lick of sense because nothing would, or could, happen with Max, I was still curious. I'd sworn off men, and for a perfectly good reason. I had an unerring accuracy for being attracted to men who were assholes. One after another stomped on my heart, the most recent having been the most devastating.

Ivy looked at me, her eyes taking on a gleam as a slight grin curled her lips. "Max is a hot one, isn't he? He's known Owen forever, since MIT, and—"

She was cut off when Owen approached, sliding his arm around her waist and dipping his head to drop a kiss on her neck.

My heart pinged. I was so happy for her. Owen loved Ivy to pieces.

"We're supposed to cut the cake," he said with a sigh.

Ivy pushed off the bar. "Now? Why are there so many rules about weddings?" she asked, looking to me as if I had the answer.

I shrugged. "Don't ask me."

Owen chuckled. "I'm told if we don't do it soon, they'll need to move it back into the kitchen."

I followed them, meandering over to stand behind the guests surrounding the table where the cake was displayed, and I caught myself searching for Max. I wanted to know more about him, and that was bad, because when I got curious about a man, I tended to do stupid things. Just as I was telling myself it was a good thing he wasn't around, all of a sudden, he strolled up beside me.

Try as I might, I couldn't keep from sneaking glances at him. He was obscenely handsome, with his midnight black hair and ice-blue eyes. I wanted to dive in and take a swim. He held a glass of scotch in his hand. Even his hands were sexy, strong, and slightly rugged, as if he'd worked with them. My mind flashed to a vision of his hands on my body, heat flooding through me in response.

Needing to direct my thoughts elsewhere, I took a gulp of my martini. *Big mistake.* I felt a different kind of burn as the alcohol traveled down my throat, and I started coughing.

"You okay?" Max asked.

His voice was low and sent a shiver over my skin. I tried to say I was fine, but I just kept coughing. His hand slid down my spine. With my dress open at the top, his touch sent fire shimmering under the surface of my skin.

My coughing outburst was drawing attention. He turned, guiding me away from the small crowd gathered around Ivy and Owen, and walked me back to the bar where Garrett was now serving drinks. Max paused at the corner of the bar, near the windows. His hand remained on my back, the heat of his touch filtering through the silk of my dress. After a few minutes, I finally managed to stop coughing.

Glancing up, I found his blue-eyed gaze watching me. "Went down the wrong pipe?" he asked.

With a sigh and another breath, I nodded, my eyes watering. I set my martini down, then reached over to snag a bar napkin and began dabbing at the lingering tears. "I'm not fit for company at things like this," I said with a little laugh.

Max was quiet for a beat and then his mouth hitched at the corner. Oh sweet hell, he should *not* smile. My belly felt funny and slivers of desire spun through my veins. He looked away, glancing over his shoulder toward the cake cutting. "I think we missed the fun."

I chuckled. "The most important part already happened."

"How long are you staying?" he asked, his gaze swinging back to me.

His question took me off guard. "I'm at the hotel until tomorrow. You?"

He shrugged. "Don't know. It's beautiful here."

As I looked up at him, my body—my traitorous body—sent naughty thoughts through my mind. The view of Max was quite beautiful. Yet, I knew that wasn't what he was talking about. I managed to keep those thoughts safely in my head, nodding politely. "It is."

Garrett joined us where we stood at the bar. I'd been here two days now, and met most everyone in Ivy and Owen's circle. I'd quickly come to learn that the Hamilton family was comprised of beautiful people. Garrett was no exception with his glossy dark hair and blue eyes. His gaze was sharp and assessing as he looked between us.

"Another drink?" he asked, his eyes flicking to my almost empty martini glass.

"Yes, please," I said quickly. I needed something to take the edge off. Having Max nearby made me restless and tingly all over.

"You?" Garrett asked, his eyes shifting to Max.

Max shook his head. "All set, but thanks. I'm the shuttle, so no more drinks for me."

Garrett chuckled as he prepped another pomegranate martini for me.

The rest of the evening was a blur. I drank too many martinis, danced, and felt the burn of Max's gaze on me every time our eyes collided. I wanted him. Badly.

Even in my tipsy state, I kept reminding myself that whenever I wanted someone, it was usually a bad decision on my part. I didn't do casual well. I never had.

I tended to fall hard and fast, getting attached and confusing attraction for something else. My therapist, the one I saw after my last relationship blew up in my face, had gently pointed out that perhaps I was looking for the affection I'd never gotten from my father.

I'd been looking high and low for love most of my life. With my mother gone, and a father who approached parenting as something to pencil in on his calendar and hand off to others, I'd craved it for too long. As such, I often misinterpreted cues and read far too much into small gestures.

Max was particularly tempting with his dark hair and the strong lines of his face, but it was his eyes that held me captive. One look from those cool blue pools, and it felt as though he was undressing me, his gaze lighting little fires on my skin everywhere they landed.

Somewhere along the way, I ended up in his arms out on the deck. Seeing as he was one of the groomsmen, and I was a bridesmaid, it only made sense we would dance at some point. Not many men enjoyed dancing, but Max surprised me. While he gave off a somber, controlled air, he danced like a dream, twirling me easily around the deck. When the music shifted into a slower song, he pulled me close, just when I was thinking I needed to make my escape.

With the heat of desire sliding through my veins and the feel of his strong embrace, my body reassured my mind that it wouldn't hurt to enjoy it for a few minutes. He smelled good, crisp, and musky, all at once. My head barely reached his shoulder, so I was pressed against Max's chest, his scent consuming me. With one of his hands gripping mine and the other splayed on my lower back, his fingers teasing over my bottom, I could feel the moisture building between my thighs, the silk of my panties wet. *This is* such *a bad idea.*

"So, Harlow, tell me what you do?" he murmured.

A rather common question, and perfectly expected. Yet, these questions were loaded for me because they reminded me of how I let my father down, over and over again.

I shoved those thoughts aside and replied, "I'm a hotshot firefighter. I finished my training last year."

Max's steps stuttered slightly, and I couldn't help but laugh, glancing up at him. "Did I surprise you?"

His eyes canted down to mine, and my breath caught in my throat as butterflies spun in my belly. This man was too much.

He was quiet for a beat, his gaze searching mine as a slow grin stretched across his face. "Yes, you surprised me."

Between his grin and the slightly rough edge to his voice, a shiver ran through me. I ordered my mind to ignore the crazy signals of my body.

Manners, Harlow. Use your manners.

"And what do you do?" I managed to ask.

I felt the shrug of his shoulders, the motion making me aware of his muscled chest pressing against my breasts. My nipples tightened, giving me away. He appeared to be considering his words.

"Business," was all he finally said.

I was just tipsy enough to be less than polite. "Vague much?"

He smiled again, sending my belly into a series of flips. "I'd rather not think about work tonight."

The song ended and a more upbeat song began. When Max stepped back, I felt bereft. My body nearly followed him, like a magnet to his steel, but I managed to stop myself. Conveniently, Ginger Nash, Ivy's sister-in-law, was approaching with two glasses in her hands.

"Champagne?" she asked, pausing at my side.

Ginger was funny and smart. Her brown hair was up in a twist, and her blue eyes were twinkling. She squeezed my arm as I accepted the proffered drink and took a gulp.

"I'm so glad you're here," she said with a wide smile. Ginger seemed to have decided we were best buddies, even though we'd only met days ago. She was easy to be around though, with her sly sense of humor and warmth.

She glanced to Max, arching a brow. "Aren't you handsome?"

Max barely reacted, his lips quirking.

"Oh, don't worry. I wasn't flirting. Just making an observation. I'm happily married," Ginger said dismissively.

Max merely arched a brow this time, his eyes glinting with mirth.

"It's a wedding, though," she continued. "Maybe you should find someone to sweep off her feet."

Max threw his head back with a laugh just as Cam Nash, Ivy's brother and Ginger's husband, approached. Cam was a totally nice guy, and quite dreamy. He'd retired from being a world-class skier and was now an instructor here at the lodge.

Cam slipped his arm around Ginger's shoulders, nodding in my direction and grinning at Max. "Ignore Ginger. She always wants to set everyone up."

Ginger nudged him with her elbow and took a sip of her champagne. "What's wrong with being romantic?"

Cam, who shared Ivy's coloring with amber hair and eyes,

cast a smile her way. "Nothing at all, but not everyone *wants* to be set up."

Unabashed, Ginger shrugged, her eyes bouncing from Max to me. "You two match. Just saying," she offered with a wink.

Chapter Three

MAX

Later that night, I pulled up in front of Midnight Sun Lodges. Glancing over to Harlow, I found her sound asleep, and I took a moment to absorb her. Her hair was mussed from the evening of dancing and socializing. Her dark lashes curled against her cheeks, and her face was relaxed in sleep, the lines of tension gone.

Harlow was all kinds of temptation. Right now, I needed to get her to her room.

After parking the car in a space close to the front entrance, I rounded it and carefully lifted her into my arms. She didn't even stiffen as I held her against my chest. She sighed softly, tucking her head against my shoulder, and my heart twisted sharply. I didn't know why Harlow affected me this way.

There was desire, but there was more under the surface. I had a burning curiosity about her. She'd shocked the hell out of me when she announced she was a firefighter. Ordering my body to behave, I carried her inside.

I had to wake her up just long enough to find out her room number, which she mumbled against my shoulder, and was out like a light again by the time we got there. I laid her down on the bed, intending to make my exit, but then I looked back at her.

Big mistake.

Her dress had ridden up around her hips, a glimpse of blue silk teasing me between her thighs, and her hair fell in a tousle on the pillows. My eyes flicked to the valley between her breasts. Just as I brought my gaze back to her face, Harlow's eyes opened and caught mine in the dim light of the hotel room.

"Don't go," she murmured.

She was tipsy, and I knew that. Yet, I couldn't seem to refuse her. Not when her stare held mine, and she beckoned me with her hand.

Next thing I knew, I'd kicked off my shoes and shrugged out of my jacket, telling myself I would stay until she fell asleep. She started to try to take her dress off, fumbling with the sleeves.

Fuck me. This was some kind of penance I didn't know I owed.

When she got it twisted around her waist, I shackled the lust rampaging through me and helped her shimmy out of her dress. She was beyond tempting in a blue silk bra and matching panties. Reminding myself she was intoxicated, I quickly yanked the covers over her.

Clinging to my restraint, I leaned against the headboard, on top of the covers, and listened as she mumbled something about hating hotels and sleeping alone. My heart gave another twist. Any kind of emotional baggage typically sent me running when it came to women, but sensing the vulnerability in Harlow only heightened my response to her. *I'll only stay until she falls asleep.*

I meant to leave.

The following morning, I came awake slowly, startled to realize I'd fallen asleep. Harlow was curled up against me. My cock was hard, my body very aware of the delectable woman right there for the taking. I took a deep breath, grasping onto my control.

There weren't many situations where my control was tested, yet, just now, I nearly ached with need for her. The only problem was, Harlow was a close friend of Owen and Ivy's, and I didn't like things to be messy. Getting skin to skin with Harlow smacked of messy.

There was that, and the fact that I wanted her more fiercely than I'd wanted anyone for as long as I could remember. The only woman who'd ever called to me like this had illuminated just how shallow the idea of love could be. That woman was the reason I treated relationships almost as professional as work.

Sex was a transaction, but as much as I wanted Harlow, I couldn't quite think of her like that. I carefully shifted, intending to roll out of bed and make my exit quietly. The moment I started to move, Harlow did as well, and I felt when she came awake. She bolted upright, her eyes flying wide open. She stared at me, her cheeks turning a delectable shade of pink.

Her hair was a tangled mess, falling down and partially masking her breasts behind the blue silk of her bra. As I looked at her—*because my eyes had a fucking mind of their own*—I saw her nipples tighten, playing peekaboo with me through the dark locks of her hair.

Fuck me.

"Oh my God! What are you doing here?!" She gasped, snatching up the sheet and tucking it under her armpits.

I swung my legs off the bed, relieved I was almost fully dressed.

"Nothing happened, Harlow."

My cock strained against my fly. *Down boy.*

Harlow stood, turning with the sheet and wrapping it around her. I almost burst out laughing, but she looked so damn mad, I bit my tongue.

"Why are you here?" She stood before me, looking like a

fucking queen in a bed sheet, her gaze shooting daggers, and her cheeks rosy red.

"You fell asleep on the ride back. I carried you up, and you asked me to stay."

I raked a hand through my hair, leaning my elbows on my knees, which also bought me a moment to get my body under control. I didn't usually have this problem. But then, I didn't make it a habit to spend the night with women. I had sex, I went on dates, I even had a few long-term arrangements, but I never spent the night.

I'd broken my own rule, and I hadn't even gotten anything out of it.

"I think you should go," Harlow said, her voice tight.

I managed to get my cock under control by keeping my mind firmly on the numbers on my latest balance sheet from a company we'd recently acquired. They'd done a piss-poor job of management, so the numbers were memorable.

I stood, on the heels of a deep breath, and turned to face her again. Holy hell, she was fucking gorgeous. I'd noticed last night that she didn't even bother with makeup, not even lipstick. Her plump, pink lips were twisted sideways as she worried the bottom corner with her teeth.

My eyes were drawn there like a bee to honey, and my cock threatened to ignore my mind again. I shifted gears, keeping my eyes locked to hers and envisioning the lines of red numbers.

"I'm leaving now."

Rounding the end of the bed, I slipped my shoes on, snagged my jacket off the back of a chair, and picked up my tie.

"Thank you for the ride," she said, her voice stilted.

She seemed tense, and that only made matters worse. I would love to see all that tied-up energy let loose. I had a feeling Harlow would be wild in bed. Too bad she didn't fit my requirements. First and foremost, I wanted her too much. She was also a friend of a friend, and I didn't need the complications.

"How much longer will you be in Diamond Creek?" I asked, pausing by the door.

Harlow held my gaze. I was fairly certain she didn't notice the sheet was pulled tight across her breasts, and that I could see the tight points of her nipples. I didn't think she would appreciate me filling her in on that tidbit, so I kept my mouth shut and my eyes on hers.

"Maybe a few days. You?"

"Same. I suppose I'll see you at the lodge then."

She nodded tightly. "I'll be up later for the breakfast."

I bit back the urge to ask her if she wanted a ride, and as I left the hotel, I decided it might be best if I steered clear of Harlow. She was much too tempting.

Chapter Four

HARLOW

A few days after the wedding, I rolled my rental car to a stop in front of Ivy and Owen's house, having decided to take Ivy up on her offer to stay at their place. Aside from craving the peace and quiet, I planned to follow up on a job lead. A position had opened up on a hotshot firefighting team in a town a few hours north of here.

I needed something to help me cut loose from my father. Being within his vicinity made it difficult to withstand his constant criticism, even though I had no doubts about what I wanted. I didn't want to work for his company. All he cared about was money. The only reason he wanted me to work for him was to control what happened to it after he died.

I wanted no part of it.

When he'd learned I'd completed my hotshot training last year, he'd scoffed at me. You'd think he might have wondered what I was up to for a year out in Montana, but he traveled so much, he rarely knew what anyone other than himself was doing. I could've already been working, but events had sent my life skidding sideways.

I was finally ready to pull my life back together. Maybe

becoming a hotshot firefighter was half-crazy, but I loved it. I loved the hard work, the immersion in the wilderness, and how strong it made me feel. I doubted I could do it forever, it wasn't that kind of job, but I couldn't rely on my father for support. I didn't want his money, I just wanted to be free of him. A job in a town about five thousand miles away might do the trick.

Climbing out of the car, I snagged my bag out of the trunk and dug in my purse for the keys. I fit the key in the lock to the side door, only to discover it was already unlocked. With a laugh, I let myself in. Kicking off my shoes, I dropped the keys on the coffee table before tossing my bag on the sofa. Their home was all space and light and comfort. It was an octagonal shape, the middle floor where you entered wide open, with the exception of a door to the bathroom and laundry room at the back. The kitchen occupied one side with a curved island counter facing the living room. The master bedroom took up the entire upstairs of the home.

I meandered downstairs to leave my bag in the guest room and returned upstairs to ascertain if I needed to make a trip to the store. Ivy had assured me I should help myself to what they had. The kitchen was well-stocked, so I could settle in for now.

After a quick shower, I elected for nothing but comfort. No one was here to see me, so I could wear whatever I wanted. That consisted of a long T-shirt that hung just past my hips, underwear, and fuzzy socks. I felt like I was living on borrowed time. I had a lovely home, with a spectacular view of the mountains and ocean, all to myself. Heaven.

I snagged a bottle of wine from the wine rack, reminding myself to restock it before I left, then set to work making myself a quick dinner. After I ate, I grabbed my glass of wine and stood by the windows, taking in the magnificent view. The mountains were stark against the sky as the sun slid down the horizon, leaving streaks of scarlet and purple in its wake. Taking a deep breath, I let it out slowly. The tension I'd been carrying was finally starting to unwind.

Alaska might be just what I need to make a definitive break.

"Excuse me," a low voice said from behind me, and I nearly dropped my glass.

A prickle of awareness ran up my spine. I knew that voice—low, gravelly, and oh-so-sexy. Heat bloomed over the surface of my skin and then it occurred to me that I was close to naked. *This isn't happening.* I spun around, my eyes widening the moment they locked with Max's gaze.

His eyes narrowed. "Harlow, what are you doing here?"

"Ivy invited me to stay," I stammered, wishing like hell I wasn't slightly tipsy from several glasses of wine.

Of course, it just *had* to be Max who encountered me like this. I'd seen more of him over the last few days after the wedding. Yet, I'd always been fully-clothed and managed to keep a casual distance. *Well, except for that one night, Harlow.* I inwardly cringed. *Shut up, brain, you aren't helping.*

Today, he wore jeans and a jersey shirt, and the faded cotton caressed his muscled chest. My eyes flew to the expanse of skin showing where the three buttons at the top were open. His skin was burnished gold. That one little spot was positively lickable.

His jeans hung low on his hips. As he lifted a hand to run it through his hair, his shirt rode up, revealing the delineated muscles at his waist. My mouth watered, and my panties were instantly damp.

"What are you doing here?"

Brilliant, Harlow, just parrot his question.

"Owen invited me to stay," he said, his gravelly voice sending another shiver chasing over the surface of my skin.

He let his bag slide free from his hand where it fell to the floor with a thump. I gave myself a mental shake. Just looking at him had heat coiling in my belly.

"Oh," I finally managed to say.

My conversational skills seemed limited by his presence.

Slightly fuzzy from the wine and my body betraying me, I needed to get a grip fast.

"Um..."

Yet again, my conversational prowess was proven when I couldn't form more than a single syllable. His gaze flicked down over my body before meandering back up, too slowly for my comfort. My nipples perked up at his perusal. I fairly burned with need from nothing more than a look from him.

"I suppose Ivy and Owen didn't chat about this," Max said with a wry grin when his eyes finally made their way back to mine.

I stayed silent, because I knew Ivy had told Owen I would be staying for a week. I wondered just what they were up to.

"I can get out of your hair," I finally said.

Max started walking in my direction, his stride slow and purposeful. With every step, my channel clenched and my belly fluttered, spinning wildly. My breasts felt tight and achy, and my pulse went wild.

I take it back. I know exactly *what Ivy and Owen are up to.*

Chapter Five

MAX

Walking toward Harlow, my mind considered two courses of action. One would be for me to do the sane thing and leave. *Now.*

The other would be for me to do precisely what I wanted —give in to the urges I'd been beating back for three long days. Because I wanted Harlow. With such ferocity, I could hardly bear it.

Her eyes were wide, her cheeks flushed, and her lips stained red from the wine she held in her hand. Her complete lack of artifice was so refreshing; she seemed oblivious to how beautiful she was. Her T-shirt hung just past her hips, and she wore a pair of bulky wool socks that reached halfway up her calves. Though her T-shirt was loose, it didn't do a damn thing to hide her assets, so to speak.

The fabric stretched across her breasts, her nipples pressing against it. Lust cracked its whip, the bite of it tightening every fiber within me.

One look at her, and I was on fire. I made a calculated decision. Even though Harlow was a friend of one of my best friends, the likelihood our paths would cross again was slim. If she worked for her father, I might have had to worry about encountering her, but apparently, she was a firefighter. I didn't even know what the hell to think of that.

I calculated three days tangled up with Harlow might be enough to burn the need to ashes.

When I reached her, her breath hitched slightly. My eyes flicked down to see her pulse fluttering in her neck. The urge to dip my head and drag my tongue along the soft skin there and taste the hint of honey and vanilla drifting to me was almost overpowering.

I gave myself a mental shake, attempting to shackle the need pounding through me. As if she could read my thoughts, her rich brown eyes darkened.

"I have an idea," I said.

"What's that?"

"I doubt our paths will ever cross again. I want you, and you want me."

Her cheeks flushed a deeper shade of pink. "I don't..."

Her words trailed off as I held her gaze. "I'm a gentleman. I won't do anything you don't want. But I think it's silly to deny the obvious."

I might not have known Harlow very well, but I sensed steel underneath her quiet exterior. The air around us heated, fairly crackling with the force of the desire between us. I wasn't prone to fanciful thinking, but I wouldn't have been surprised if sparks scattered around us.

Harlow took a gulp of her wine. Anger flashed in her eyes, and my cock strained against my fly.

"I wasn't going to deny the obvious," she finally said, resting her free hand on her hip, conveniently hitching her T-shirt up just enough to reveal the curve of her hip. "But that doesn't mean I want to do anything about it."

She was a sensible woman. I was a sensible man. Usually.

In this moment, however, rational thought was hard to find. The only thing I hoped to do just now was persuade her not to worry about the future—to agree with me on this foolish gamble. We could burn this to ashes and walk away unscathed.

Before I realized what I was doing, I lifted a hand, brushing a loose lock of hair away from her forehead and tucking it behind her ear. I felt the shiver that ran through her, my own body tightening in response.

"I'm simply proposing a clean, three-day window. Just us. We'll let this play out and then walk away. That's it. I won't lie. I don't do relationships. If you're worried about that, there's no need."

Harlow stared at me, her lips parting slightly, her tongue darting out to swipe across her bottom lip. I wished I could see into her mind. I didn't usually give a damn what anyone was thinking. With Harlow, I did. I wanted to know what made her tick.

Walking away from her father's business didn't make sense. Being a firefighter didn't either. But then, in a way, it did. I could sense her strength and an edge of recklessness to her. I sensed she tried to keep herself buttoned up tight, and I wanted to set her loose. She took another gulp of wine, turning quickly and striding away. As if an invisible thread attached me to her, I reflexively followed.

"Well?"

Her breath hitched again. All she had to do was breathe, and I wanted her so fiercely, I ached.

"Okay," she said softly.

That was all I needed. I caught the dark fall of her hair in my hand, winding it around my fist. Stepping closer, I came flush against her back, almost groaning aloud when the achingly hard length of my cock fit between the cheeks of her lush bottom. Her head fell back against my shoulder.

Dusting kisses along her neck, her skin pebbled under my lips. A soft moan escaped when I dragged my tongue along the same path.

She stiffened and then pushed away, spinning to face me.

Her hair slipped loose from my hand as her heated gaze collided with mine.

"A few ground rules," I said, as I stared into Max's eyes and scrambled for purchase inside my mind and body.

Making eye contact was downright dangerous. Hell, *he* was downright dangerous.

Max met my eyes and arched a brow. That was all it took to send another wash of heat through me, and flutters spinning in my belly. Being close to him made me feel half-crazy. It felt as if the air around us was alive, shimmering with desire. It was hard to imagine Max wanted me as much as I wanted him, but the look in his eyes told a different story. His gaze was dark and so intent, it took my breath away.

I was simply standing there, staring at him, when he arched his brow a little higher, his mouth curling at the corner in a grin, promptly sending my belly into a flip.

What was I saying? Rules, right. I said we needed ground rules.

They were more for me than him. I was already in over my head. My tendency to want to be wrapped in someone's strength, my fascination with falling in love—those urges were fierce.

This attraction ran too deep, a force I couldn't resist.

"Ground rules," I repeated. I meant to speak firmly, but my voice came out husky.

I straightened my shoulders and felt, rather than saw, his gaze flick down to my breasts. My nipples tightened further, perking up and all but begging on my behalf. I felt my cheeks heat when his eyes raised again, a gleam of mirth there.

"Please tell me the ground rules, Harlow."

Every time he said my name, it felt as if he was making love to it. Slightly gruff and low, his voice sent a shiver through me.

"Not three nights, one night."

This rule went against everything I wanted, but I couldn't let myself have more.

It felt as if Max could see straight through my bullshit. He cocked his head to the side. "Maybe."

"Maybe?" I rested a hand on my hip, narrowing my eyes and attempting to look stern. "That's one of my rules. One night."

His smile was slow and devastating. "If you still say the same thing tomorrow morning, then you have my word."

Oh, he was so arrogant!

"How do I know you're a man of your word?"

Despite my annoyance, I was enjoying this. With heat blooming through me, acutely aware of the moisture between my thighs, I lifted my chin.

Max chuckled. "Owen is one of my best friends. If you know him well, which I understand you do, then you can trust my word. Feel free to call him and verify."

Despite my misgivings about the state of my heart, and my tendency to fall head over heels in love with men who were terrible for me, I trusted Max. For the very reason he noted.

"Fine."

"No need to call to verify?" he countered.

I shook my head.

"Any more ground rules?"

"This is a one-time thing."

Max nodded solemnly. "I'm not guessing our paths will cross again. If they do, there will be no expectations. Anything else?"

Need coiled tightly in my core, anticipation fairly vibrating through me. I shook my head. I didn't have any more rules, but now the moment was upon us. Simply having Max close to me nearly made me burst into flames.

He reached out, catching my hand in his, and closed the distance between us. When the heat and strength of his body came against mine, my pulse took off like a rocket. My breath came in shallow pants as need spun through my veins.

"Harlow," he said.

He threaded a hand into my hair, sliding it down to cup the nape of my neck. Goose bumps chased over my skin in the wake of his touch.

Then, his lips were on mine. I couldn't say what I had expected, but I suppose I expected him to dominate instantly. In a way, he did, but not in the way I imagined. The moment his lips met mine, a jolt of electricity shot through me, striking me at my core.

His touch was just a brush of his lips against mine. He kissed one corner of my mouth and then the other, effectively wiping away my defenses. His tongue swiped across my lips and swept into my mouth. He still gripped one of my hands, but slid his other palm down my spine and over my bottom, palming it and rocking his arousal into me.

He was fully clothed, while I wore practically nothing. I should have felt vulnerable. I did, but not in the way I expected. My heart was instantly at risk; my tricky, oh-so-wishful heart savored his strength and the depth of need burning between us.

With his tongue tangling with mine, the feel of his arousal hard and hot at the apex of my thighs, a surge of power rolled through me. That this man could want me this boldly was a heady sensation. When he drew back slightly, catching my bottom lip in his teeth, I tried to grab onto some semblance of control as I gulped in air.

"Harlow," he murmured, his gruff voice sending goose bumps prickling over my skin again.

Opening my eyes, I found his gaze waiting, the icy blue darkened to a rich sapphire. His gaze was so intense, I couldn't look away.

I tried to catch my breath, managing to murmur, "Yes?"

He loosened his hand in my hair, tracing along my collarbone, and then dipping to cup one of my breasts through my T-shirt, my nipples tightening so much they ached. His thumb brushed over one, and I couldn't hold back the low moan that escaped. I shifted my legs restlessly, which only served to heighten the need knotted at the apex of my thighs.

"Now would be the time to tell me you don't want this," he finally said.

I almost laughed. I supposed I could lie blatantly and tell him I didn't want him, but with need rampaging through me and warning bells blaring, he was all I wanted.

I shook my head, moaning again with another brush of his thumb across my nipple.

"Is that a 'no,' you don't want to stop, or 'no,' you don't want this?"

He was going to make me be direct.

"I want this."

Satisfaction flared in his eyes. "Good. Because I want you," he said flatly.

His words sent another surge of power through me.

He dipped his head swiftly, closing his mouth over my nipple right through my T-shirt, the wet heat of his mouth and the friction of the fabric making me cry out. Then, his mouth was on my other nipple, and I nearly melted at his feet. When he lifted his head, I glanced down to see the tight points pressing against the damp fabric.

Everything moved swiftly after that. His hands were everywhere—cupping my bottom, sliding up under my T-shirt, the subtle abrasion of his touch against my skin sending slivers of fire under the surface.

I needed more. I slid a hand under his shirt, savoring the heat of his skin. With a low groan, I arched into the hard, hot length of his cock.

"Harlow..."

Opening my eyes, I found his waiting. He reached for the glass of wine in my hand. With a slow spin, he set it on the windowsill behind us and then lifted me against him. My legs curled reflexively around his hips.

He held me easily. In a few strides, he reached the kitchen counter and slid my hips onto it, the contrast of the cool tile against my skin merely serving to ratchet up the heat inside. He hooked a hand on the hem of my T-shirt, pulling it straight up and over my head. It sailed through the air, falling to the floor in a soft rumple.

I sat there, in nothing but my blue silk panties and a pair of socks. I felt bare as his eyes trailed down over my breasts, my nipples tightening at the feel of his gaze burning against my skin. Stepping between my knees, he cupped my breasts in his hands, teasing my tight peaks with his thumbs. "You're so beautiful, Harlow."

A small sound escaped from my throat as my hips arched into him. Freeing one of my breasts, he reached down, gripping my hip and tugging me closer to the edge of the counter.

Everything blurred. He dragged his tongue along my neck, over the dip in my throat, and then down to swirl around my nipples, his teeth scoring them lightly. Yanking at his shirt, I was relieved when he stepped back to reach behind his head and tug it off. I got a glimpse of his chest, all hard, muscled planes and burnished skin, with a smattering of dark hair that narrowed to a point.

Tearing his fly open, I reached into his jeans and curled

my hand around his cock, almost moaning at the feel of it. He made me crazy—greedy, needy, wanting everything at once. His fingers trailed over my belly and dipped between my thighs, teasing over the wet silk.

He lifted me with ease, hooking his finger over the edge of my panties and dragging them down. I kicked them free, and then he was stepping between the cage of my knees again as I freed his cock from his briefs. His fingers teased my folds, which were drenched with desire.

I didn't want to wait. I needed all of it—*now*. He buried two fingers in me, knuckle deep. I cried out, gripping his shoulders as I arched into his touch. I felt his eyes on me and wanted to look away, but I couldn't. It was as if a magnet held my gaze to his as he fucked me slowly with his fingers.

"Let go," he said softly.

On the heels of his command, he pressed his thumb down, rolling it over my clit. Pleasure unraveled in a burst, my channel clenching around his fingers as I cried out.

Inside of a hot second, while I was still coming down from the intensity of my climax, I heard the sound of a foil tearing. Dragging my eyes open, I found him rolling a condom on. His jeans hung low on his hips. He tugged me closer to the edge of the counter, teasing me with the head of his cock. Still reeling from my release, I was already spiraling inside. I needed to feel him inside me. I wanted it rough, hard, and fast.

Max gave it to me exactly how I wanted it. A few more teases, sliding back and forth through my drenched folds, and he murmured my name. The moment my eyes locked with his, he sank inside in one swift surge, filling me deeply.

It had been a full year since I'd had actual sex. I was tight, but the slight burn of him filling me was welcome. I needed it, the mingling of pleasure and pain.

Chapter Seven

MAX

Staring at Harlow, I clung to my control. She felt better than I could've even imagined—hot, slick, and so tight, I almost came from simply sinking inside of her.

I wanted to watch her fly apart again. I slid one hand down to grip her hip, holding her in place. Lifting the other, I brushed her hair back from her face, savoring her shiver. Running my hand through her hair and down her spine, I cupped her sweet ass, pulling her closer. When I thought I had enough control, I drew back and sank inside of her—again and again and again.

"Touch yourself," I murmured.

The words simply slipped out. Reaching between us, her finger slipped into her glistening folds, and I watched as she pressed over her pink, swollen clit. She cried out, her channel throbbing around me. My own release came swiftly, almost brutally. Heat twisted at the base of my spine and whipped through me, the pleasure so intense, my knees almost gave out.

My head fell into the dip of her shoulder as her body slowly curled into me. This should've been the point where I drew away. But I didn't, I couldn't. I wanted to stay right there, buried deep inside her, caught in the shimmering intimacy.

Harlow finally lifted her head, her eyes meeting mine. We were quiet for several beats. I wanted to know what she was thinking, and that was dangerous.

———

The following morning, I woke in the darkness. I felt Harlow's body, warm and soft, against my side. One of her legs was hooked over mine with her head tucked into my shoulder. Last night had barely taken the edge off my need. Just now, my cock swelled at the feel of her. In my sleep, I'd wrapped an arm around her, my palm cupping her lush bottom.

None of this bothered me. No, what rattled me was the clench of my heart when I tucked her against me just before she fell asleep last night. I wasn't a foolish man. Control wasn't an issue for me. Usually.

I'd thought I could have a taste of her and walk away. I needed to get out of this bed before I gave in again and let the intimacy hiding within the desire stitch us tighter and tighter together.

A few hours later, when the sun was finally coming up, my email pinged on my laptop, where I'd been working at the kitchen counter. I shouldn't have been relieved when I saw the email, but I was. I'd just been handed an excuse to leave. Nothing like an urgent business meeting to get me back on track.

Harlow came out of the bedroom as I was draining the last of my coffee. My entire body tightened at the sight of her. Her dark hair fell in a tousle and her cheeks were flushed from sleep. She wore a T-shirt and socks again, making my heart clench.

"No need to worry about ground rules," I said, as I set my empty coffee mug in the sink.

"Oh?"

"Business emergency, so the place is all yours."

She was quiet, her eyes searching my face. For a flash, my heart kicked abruptly against my ribs. I thought I saw disappointment in her gaze, and it nearly crushed me.

Precisely why I had to get the hell out of there.

A year or so later

Resting a hand on my hip, I dragged my sleeve across my face and scanned my gaze over the charred trees stretching in front of me. Turning away, I strode a few steps to a fallen log, leaning over to pick up a water bottle and draining it. In the other direction, I could see Denali in the distance, the centerpiece of the Alaskan Range. We were just finishing up a controlled burn about an hour north of Willow Brook, Alaska, where I had taken a position on a hotshot crew last year.

Being a hotshot firefighter was everything I expected and more. I had a clean break from the harsh tension between my father and me, and had immersed myself in the work. This job gave me the gift of living and breathing the outdoors. I loved the wilderness; I always had. I supposed that was because I rarely got to see it when I was growing up, bouncing from one hotel to another. My childhood schedule was entirely subject to the regimen of my father's work.

Just now, even with the scent of smoke lingering in the air and the charred section of forest we'd burned to manage a swathe of dead spruce, the beauty nearly brought me to my knees. The bright blue sky seemed endless here. The stark lines of the mountain ridges and peaks took my breath away. In another direction, wilderness stretched as far as the eye could see. It was late autumn, almost into November, with the air chilly, winter nipping to catch it in its teeth.

"Harlow!" a voice called.

Spinning around, I saw Ward Taylor, the superintendent for my crew, waving me over. We were leaving this afternoon and heading back to Willow Brook. I surmised our helicopter would be here any minute. Snagging my backpack and stuffing my water bottle into it, I slung it over my shoulder and jogged over to where Ward was waiting. The other half of our crew had flown out earlier today.

"What's up?" I asked as soon as I slowed to a stop in front of him. I liked Ward as a boss. I completely respected him, as did the rest of our crew. I supposed he could've been intimidating. Yet, he had a major soft spot. All you had to do was see him once with his wife Susannah and their baby son, and his intimidation factor dissolved. He adored them.

That said, he was tall, all muscle, and quite handsome. He and Susannah made a gorgeous pair. Her strawberry blonde hair and blue eyes were a contrast to his dark hair and silver eyes. Susannah had become a friend in the time I'd been in Willow Brook. At the moment, she was the only other female hotshot firefighter amongst the crews stationed at Willow Brook Fire & Rescue. She used to be on Ward's crew, and that was when we'd become friends; although, at the time, I'd been on a different crew. After she got pregnant, she transferred over to the local crew to manage the reality of having a baby, and I shifted into her position. There were all kinds of jobs one could do as a parent, but a job as a hotshot firefighter made it challenging if only because of the travel.

As for me, I was still footloose and fancy free. My mind started to spin in painful directions, so I forced my attention back to work. Ward had yet to answer my question, as he'd been distracted by a comment from someone else. Letting my backpack slide off my shoulder to the ground, I shook my arms loose.

Ward turned back to me. "Nate just radioed in, and he'll be out here to pick us up any minute."

As if on cue, we heard the distinct sound of a helicopter in the distance, and in a matter of minutes, it was landing. Aside from flying all over the Alaskan skies to ferry tourists, Nate Fox delivered fire retardant and water from above during fires, and occasionally ferried our crews in and out of the backcountry. Nate stepped out once the helicopter settled on to the ground, waving as he approached.

Nate stopped beside his brother, Caleb Fox, who was a foreman on my crew. He and Caleb looked so much alike, it was amusing. Both had brown hair and brown eyes and carried themselves with rugged strength and grace. Of the two, Nate was more easygoing. Nate flashed a grin at the group in general. "You guys all ready?"

Caleb arched a brow. "Of course we are, and we're fucking tired, so let's get this show on the road."

Nate merely shrugged and spun around, gesturing for us to follow. In short order, all of our gear was stowed, and Nate was easing the helicopter up into the sky. After a moment of watching the landscape roll underneath us, I leaned my head back against the seat, thinking about the hot shower to come.

There wasn't much that could be more heavenly than a shower after a few weeks out in the backcountry. No amount of luxury could hold a candle to it. All I wanted was to get warm and clean. By no means had this been a long stint— we'd only been out for a week—but it had been grueling work. We were taking care of some controlled burns before winter hit. Quick icy dips in rivers and streams weren't quite the same as a steaming hot shower to ease the aches born of pushing your body to its limits, day in and day out.

My life right now was such a far cry from what I had ever experienced that sometimes I didn't know what to think. When I had time to reflect, my mind spun in a certain direction, the path a well-worn groove. Far more often than I liked to let myself contemplate, Max Channing danced along the edges of my thoughts. Well, that didn't quite capture it. He commanded center stage of every fantasy I had. I'd had enough orgasms on account of the mere thought of that man to make me blush.

Every single one of them paled in comparison to the real thing, though, and I was fairly convinced Max had permanently ruined me for any other man. That was something, coming from me. I was prone to wishing and hoping when it came to men. Wishful should've been my middle name. Just now, my mind started down that path. Max would probably run screaming if he saw me now. With a mental shake, I scolded my naughty thoughts, lifted my head, and stared out at the mountains rolling underneath the helicopter.

———

Later that evening, I pushed through the door into the entryway, stopping by the reception and dispatch counter at Willow Brook Fire & Rescue. Maisie Steele was laughing at something, her dark curls bouncing as she shook her head. Leaning against the counter circling Maisie, Susannah arced her eyes in my direction, shrugging sheepishly.

"I'm not as good at this 'mom' thing as Maisie is. I swear, I can't get Wayne to sleep through the night. I feel like a complete failure," Susannah said.

Maisie's gaze sobered. "You're not a failure. Max took almost a year before he slept through the night. Carol's easier, and I don't really know why," she commented, referring to her toddler and baby, respectively.

Susannah sighed, her eyes looking tired. "It's easier when we can take turns getting up."

"Well, Ward's back now," I offered.

Susannah smiled softly. "I know. I didn't plan very well because tonight is card night."

Maisie grinned. "I think you should skip tonight. In fact"—her gaze swung to me—"why don't you come?"

Maisie was the dispatcher for Willow Brook Fire & Rescue, and she was becoming a friend, along with Susannah. I'd been here about a year now, and I was slowly starting to fit into the community. Sometimes I felt like I needed Social Skills Training 101. I'd never really been in one place for any length of time, so becoming part of a community like this was new for me. So was having friends. With most of my childhood spent with adults, I hadn't had too many friends. Ivy was my best friend, and that just seemed lucky. Our friendship had formed quickly, and though we talked and texted regularly, we'd never lived in the same place.

This whole situation was brand new to me—living in one place, trying to find my own skin, so to speak, beyond the limits of the life my father had wanted for me, which I'd soundly rejected.

I belatedly realized Maisie and Susannah were patiently waiting for me to respond. "I don't think so," I finally said.

"Well, you need to start coming," Maisie said firmly. "And Susannah, you need to go home and be with Ward tonight. I know how that is. I mean..." She paused, cutting her gaze to the door that led into the back of the station. "Beck is pretty awesome when he gets home." Her words trailed off, and her cheeks flushed.

Susannah giggled, her own cheeks turning pink. Beck was Maisie's husband and served as foreman on a different hotshot crew. I connected the dots and gathered they were talking about sex. This kind of girl talk was something I'd only ever had with Ivy.

Of late, it had been gnawing at me that I was keeping a

bit of a secret from her. I didn't suppose I *had* to tell her about what happened with Max, but it felt odd that she didn't know and it had been over a year ago now. He was a close friend of Owen's and, by extension, her. I had a habit of foolishly flinging myself into relationships, thinking everyone was the true love of my life. Ivy knew of my last breakup, which wasn't even recent anymore. It was over two years ago, and it had been brutal. Lately, she'd been telling me I needed to stop *sequestering* myself. Her word, not mine. I didn't think it was quite that, but more that I hadn't met anyone who interested me.

Except Max.

When it came to my last relationship, I'd once again fallen into fantasy love with a man completely emotionally unavailable. Nothing new there. To add to the emotional destruction, in spite of birth control, I got pregnant and ended up having a miscarriage. The very same week I lost the baby, I learned the man I thought I loved had been sleeping around. Debasing me even further, he'd felt the need to clarify it wasn't cheating. Not in his mind, at least, because he'd never told me we were exclusive, never told me he loved me. No, I'd just spun fantasies in my head and wished for so much more.

Ivy didn't know about my wild one-night stand with Max. Oh, she'd asked about him, and I was still convinced she had secretly plotted to throw us together at their house. When she brought him up, I'd answered vaguely and told her he had to leave for a business trip.

Anyway, I digress. Girlfriends talking about sex and babies. It was all very bittersweet for me.

"Please say you'll come. It'll be fun, and it's low-key," Maisie said brightly. If she'd noticed that I'd zoned out for a minute or so, it didn't show.

I looked over at her with her wild brown curls, her doe-like brown eyes, and plump cheeks with freckles scattered across them, and considered that she might be the most adorable person I'd ever seen. She was just plain cute. She insisted to me that she used to be a cranky bitch and declared she still had to work on her attitude. Here and there, I caught glimpses of her alleged attitude, but it was rare. She loved her job and adored her husband and children. Meanwhile, Beck worshipped the ground she walked on. He loved her in a way I would've sold my soul to have, but I'd largely figured wasn't in the cards for me.

Maisie's warm plea was hard to resist, no matter how hard I tried, and I felt myself nodding.

It'll be practice. You can make friends.

Later that evening, I found myself at Maisie and Beck's house. Aside from Maisie, there were four other women there: Amelia Masters, Lucy Phillips, Charlie Lane, and Ella Masters. Amelia and Lucy ran a construction company together. Charlie was a doctor, and Ella was an environmental researcher. At a glance, they all intimidated me, yet everyone was nice and welcoming.

I hadn't prepared myself for the way my heart would feel as we played cards and chatted casually. While Maisie held her little boy Max on her lap, crazy things happened in my heart. Ever since my miscarriage, I often calculated how old my baby would've been if she'd lived. I had no idea if my baby would have been a girl, but my heart thought she was. Max was almost eighteen months, and I couldn't help but think if I'd had my little girl, she'd be about a year older than him. Seeing Max and Carol made me long for the baby I'd lost. Carol was whisked off to bed by Beck right after I arrived, which had been a relief because seeing younger babies was almost painful sometimes.

Buckle up, Harlow. This is your life, and it's much better than it was before. You have a job you love. You're on your own, living in an amazing place, and you're making friends. That's more than most people ever have. So count your blessings and get over it.

My mind flashed to that one night and the way it felt to be with Max, the intimacy almost searing my soul. That had to be a trick, or so I kept telling myself. It was just me being me, believing in something that wasn't even there. I hadn't heard from Max since that night. I reminded myself, time and time again, that our lives were worlds apart.

Chapter Nine

MAX

"No," I said firmly, leaning back in my chair.

I spun away from my desk to look out the window at the city of San Francisco, where my company's home office was located. After my days at MIT, I'd done some engineering work here and there, and eventually founded a small design firm here, focused on sustainable energy products. It had grown by leaps and bounds since then, and I rarely did the actual engineering work myself these days. I'd always been good with numbers and ended up shifting into more of an investor in other firms over time, the very topic of my current conversation.

"Seriously, Max?" Owen asked.

Usually when I said no, people didn't question it. But Owen did. Every damn time. I chuckled as I looked across the skyline of San Francisco to the Golden Gate Bridge in the distance.

"Of course I'm serious," I replied, spinning my chair back around and rolling my eyes at the computer screen. We were on a videoconference call, something we did almost weekly.

Owen laughed. "I don't think you are. It's a great opportunity, and we should snap it up while we can. There are a few patents I'd like to have in our hands."

Owen ran Off the Grid, a small, but high-profile, sustainable energy company in Alaska. Our friendship from MIT and our intersecting businesses had led to multiple business collaborations. We shared a few engineers and occasionally bought up floundering companies together. That was the purpose of our call today, or rather, Owen had made it about that.

"All right, fine," I said. "But if we're doing this, we're doing it now. Say, by next week."

Owen grinned. "Perfect. So you'll fly up then?" He looked away from the screen, glancing over his shoulder. Looking back to me, he added, "Ivy's here."

Within seconds, Ivy was leaning down to smile at me, waving. "Hey, Max. Did I just hear you saying yes to Owen?"

"Of course you did. You know him, he browbeat me into it."

I teased, but Owen had good judgment, which was usually why he could talk me into things.

Ivy laughed, leaning over and dropping a kiss on Owen's cheek. "It's a smart move. I looked into the designs they have, and there's some really good stuff there."

Owen nodded and slipped his arm around her waist. "Okay, babe. Before you get going on all the designs, remember I've got a meeting in five minutes."

Ivy loved, absolutely *loved*, talking engineering and diving into the details. Being one of the best engineers in the field of sustainable energy meant she could wax poetic on the topic most of the time. Owen knew her well, and was definitely heading her off at the pass.

"Okay, okay," she said with a low laugh as she stepped back. Looking to me again, she asked, "Does that mean you'll come to Diamond Creek when you're up here in Anchorage next week?"

"Is it just me, or were you counting on me saying yes?" I asked, directing my question to Owen.

Owen grinned. "I was banking on it. It's a good plan."

Ivy rephrased her question. "So you'll come to Diamond Creek?"

A vision of Harlow May flashed in my mind. It had been a year or so since I'd seen her. Not that I would admit it to anyone, but I'd thought about her almost every day since. The last time I'd been to Diamond Creek, I'd seen her. That woman had burrowed herself into my brain and seared her memory into my mind and body. Oh, I wasn't so foolish as to let myself think anything could come of it. No matter how much I wanted to see Harlow again.

In fact, I'd stuck to my usual ways. I had a few perfectly casual business-like relationships that met my physical needs, so to speak. Yet, nothing seemed able to slake my need anymore. Were it not for the fact that I knew the women I saw wanted nothing more from me, I would worry I was using them. Well, to be blunt, I was. But it was a two-way street, so I felt no guilt. Every fucking time I left—because I didn't stay the night with anyone—I thought of Harlow and how I had slept in the same bed with her, not only once, but twice. Once, a perfectly chaste night. The other? The hottest fucking night of my life.

Harlow had ruined me for anyone else.

I hadn't realized I'd completely zoned out until Owen rapped his knuckles on his desk. "Max, easy question."

That was precisely how distracting Harlow was. There's no way on God's green earth that I would admit to Owen that half the reason I'd been hesitant to agree to his request that we snap up this alternative energy company in Anchorage was because I was actually afraid I might cross paths with Harlow again.

What terrified me was how fiercely I wanted to see her.

Giving my head a shake, I caught Owen's eyes and shrugged. "Sorry about that. Got distracted by some voices in the hallway. To your question, Ivy, it sounds like I'll be up next week. Of course I'll come to Diamond Creek."

Ivy squealed and clapped her hands. "Perfect!"

"Don't get me wrong, I'll be really glad to see you, but what's so perfect about it?"

"We're having a thing next weekend. You guys can do your meeting in Anchorage, and then come down for the weekend," she explained.

"What's a *thing*?" I asked in return.

She rolled her eyes and shrugged. "It's an after-Thanksgiving, before-Christmas thing at the ski lodge, and we'd love for you to be there. I worry about you."

Owen nodded, catching my eyes with a rueful grin. "She does worry about you. She wants to be everybody's mother."

Ivy rolled her eyes and kicked Owen's knee with her foot. "I don't want to be your mother, but I don't like thinking about you going to business meetings on Christmas Eve. Stay for a month, or more, so you're here for Christmas. Please."

"I don't know how long I'll be there, but it will definitely be a few weeks. As it is, we've got a mess to clean up. I'll head to Alaska after I fly home to see my family for Thanksgiving. You don't really need to worry about me. If I happen to be working on Christmas Eve, it's because I have to."

"Oh whatever. You're as bad as Owen is, always working. You remember Harlow, right?" Ivy asked next.

Jesus fucking Christ. I was starting to wonder if Ivy had telepathic skills.

Keeping that thought to myself, I replied blandly. "Of course I remember her. She was at your wedding, and then you guys accidentally booked both of us at your house after you left."

Not even Owen knew what happened between Harlow and me.

Ivy laughed. "That was a failed effort on my part to set

you two up. But it didn't work. Harlow said you didn't even stay, that you left for business."

I filed that detail away. I wasn't quite sure how to interpret the fact that Harlow hadn't said a word to Ivy about what happened in the single night I'd been there.

"Anyway, lots of people will be here. So are you flying into Anchorage or Homer?" she asked.

"I haven't even booked my flights yet, Ivy. I just said yes to Owen a minute before you came in the room. I'll probably fly into Anchorage. I love the drive down Turnagain Arm. Plus, if we're going to do this, we need to move fast, so I'll spend a little time in Anchorage before I go to Diamond Creek."

Satisfied, Ivy beamed, quickly leaning over to drop another kiss on Owen's cheek. Hurrying out of the room, she called over her shoulder that she would see me next weekend.

Owen and I got down to the details after that. The company in question was struggling financially. They had overstretched significantly. We would buy it up at a bargain price, at a time when they probably would see us as a lifeboat out of the nightmare situation they'd created. We were buying up a troubled alternative energy company in Anchorage. They had good ideas, but they spent money too fast without bringing enough in to balance out the risk. Owen wanted the patents to their designs. Even though I'd initially said no, it was a smart move. Except for the fact that I'd be in the vicinity of the one woman I hadn't been able to forget.

Owen and I went way back to our days together at MIT. We complemented each other in business. I did more numbers, while he did more design. There were few business partners I trusted the way I trusted Owen.

I told myself that perhaps seeing Harlow would kick her to the curb in my mind. I'd probably made her into more than she was in my memory. I had never done any online sleuthing about a woman. Until Harlow. I hadn't been able to help myself. I knew she'd taken a firefighter position in a town slightly northwest of Anchorage in Alaska. Her career choice was still a mystery to me. She'd turned down her father's attempt to pull her into his company, cutting all ties financially with him. He'd publicly disowned her as a result.

Her choice to break away from him wasn't a surprise, not to me. I hated thinking she didn't have a family, though. With a mental shake, I stood from my desk, shrugging on my suit jacket and leaving. I ran the company, so I could do whatever the hell I wanted with my schedule. In days gone by, that would've meant I was here from the crack of dawn until hours after the sun went down and not minding it a bit. My schedule remained largely the same, with a few exceptions. I was restless and antsy, though, and needed to get out of the office.

The city was like an ill-fitting jacket for me. I'd made the decisions I had in my career that relied on me being in more urban centers. Now I was at a place where I could do whatever the hell I wanted.

Harlow aside, Alaska was quite appealing. Owen had made a brilliant move when he relocated Off the Grid there. In the online world, location wasn't as important as it once was. Once you had the connections in place, you could work pretty much anywhere.

Harlow had been a source of great distraction for me. I didn't like contemplating that she had actually figured in my initial resistance to Owen's plan that we buy up this company in Anchorage. It was a smart business move, and I damn well knew it. With Harlow in Alaska, the reality I might actually see her again was an unholy temptation and not good for my sanity. I wasn't used to wanting someone the way I wanted her.

I left the office, swung by my place to change, and headed to a nearby park for a grueling run. When I needed to clear my mind, I exercised. As such, even though I'd been in good shape when I met Harlow, the elapsing year had put me in the best shape of my life.

Today, even though I ran at a punishing pace, the idea of seeing her again teased the edges of my thoughts the entire time. I hadn't been celibate since I'd seen Harlow, but she was unforgettable.

Maybe, just maybe, seeing Harlow would actually get her out of my thoughts. I'd been trying to convince myself that the memory of what I felt with her was more powerful than the reality.

Ha. You wish. You're scared of her. Because she made you feel something for the first time in years.

Chapter Ten

HARLOW

Snow was falling softly outside, glittering in the lights cast across the back deck at Last Frontier Lodge. I took another sip of water, turning when I heard a voice calling my name.

"There you are," Ivy said.

"Yup, right here." I stood from the table, and Ivy threw her arms around me for a big hug. She was a major hugger.

I'd come down for Thanksgiving and the following weekend, at her behest. Her parents were staying at her and Owen's place, so I was here at the ski lodge. It was simply beautiful, and somehow, it managed to feel both luxurious and almost like a home—if only because I knew most everyone who worked here through Ivy. The Hamilton family owned and managed the lodge, and they treated every employee like family.

Speaking of, Delia Hamilton came through the swinging doors from the kitchen in the back, carrying a tray with mugs of spiked hot cider as she walked over to us. Delia had situated me here at this table by the windows and close to the kitchen when I arrived earlier, assuring me Ivy would know right where to find me.

"Perfect timing," Ivy said, the moment she saw Delia. "I've been up to my eyeballs in designs today. I need a drink. Don't worry, I won't be driving home. Owen's meeting us here."

Ivy settled into the booth across from me while Delia set the drinks down in front of us. "I'll join you two in a little bit, but do you need anything else?"

"Actually, I could use a salmon burger. I forgot to eat before I left to drive here," I replied.

"I'll take one too because I forgot to eat while I was working today," Ivy added.

Delia grinned, her blue eyes twinkling. "So, two salmon burgers. Would you like those with regular fries or sweet potato fries?"

"You don't actually have to wait on us. Just..." I began, pausing when Delia shook her head.

"I would be asking you what you wanted if you were at my house, so get over it, and you're not paying for dinner," Delia ordered.

"She's bossy," a man's voice said from behind Delia.

Glancing over my shoulder, I saw Garrett Hamilton, Delia's handsome husband, approaching.

She rolled her eyes at him, just before he stepped to her side and caught her lips in a quick kiss.

"How late are you working tonight?" he asked.

"I'm putting this order in for them, and that's it."

"Perfect," he replied with a wink, and Delia spun away.

"Sweet potato fries, sweet potato fries!" Ivy called out, and Delia gave a thumbs up as she pushed through the doors back into the kitchen.

Garrett looked between us. "Can I crash the party?"

"Of course," Ivy replied with a wide smile, tucking a lock of her amber hair behind her ear. "That's why it's a big table."

Garrett slipped into a seat, and in a matter of minutes, he pulled most of my life story out of me. Garrett was easy to be around and so perceptive, it was slightly unnerving. He shared the same dark hair, paired with bright blue eyes, with most of his siblings.

I knew from Ivy he'd once been a highly successful corporate lawyer in Seattle. He'd burned out and moved up to Diamond Creek when he fell in love with Delia. He still practiced law, and I imagined he still made quite a bit of money. His teasing manner, though, was at odds with the idea of him as a corporate lawyer in a suit and tie.

Delia joined us shortly afterwards, and we nibbled on our dinners as we chatted. I was mellow and relaxed after a mug of Delia's ridiculously good hard cider, which was exactly what I needed. I saw Ivy's gaze flick behind me, a smile stretching across her face, and figured Owen was here.

"Max!"

Oh God. She couldn't mean Max Channing. My skin prickled at the back of my neck and a rush of heat rolled through me. I didn't even know if he was actually here; just the idea of him had that effect on me. I forced myself not to look over my shoulder. Not that I had to wait long. In a minute, Owen was standing beside the table with Max coming up behind him.

The moment I looked up, it was as if there was a magnetic force between the two of us. I knew that Owen was there and I should say hello, but my eyes went straight to Max. I found his gaze waiting, the ice blue of his eyes startling.

Heat flared inside, and I tried to take a breath, but I struggled to make my lungs work. It felt as if a shimmer of electricity arced between us. His eyes darkened, and he inclined his head slightly. "Hello, Harlow."

Oh, sweet Jesus. Just the sound of his voice sent my belly spinning, and an ache began to build between my thighs. I'd been telling myself for over a year that my fantasies about him towered over reality. I wasn't so sure now.

I didn't quite know how, but Max ended up seated beside

me. I felt a little crazy, giddy, with butterflies fluttering madly in my belly and my pulse skittering wildly. Somehow, I was going to have to behave like a normal human being.

Manners, Harlow. Use your manners. God, that sounds like something I've said before.

After greetings had been made and everyone was seated, Max caught my eyes. "How are you?" he asked.

A perfectly normal question to ask. Yet, the sound of his voice sent a shiver skating over my skin. I remembered that voice like it was yesterday.

I thanked the stars I could control my outward emotions even though my insides were screaming. It was unlikely anyone noticed my moment of speechlessness unless they were camped out in my brain.

"I'm fine," I finally said.

Wow. Two entire words.

They might've been short, but given how unsettled I was inside, it felt like a victory. Blessedly, someone—hell if I knew who—said something to Max, and his attention shifted away from me. Over the next few minutes, more people joined us, as Garrett's sister-in-law Marley and her husband Gage slipped into chairs. As conversation flowed, it occurred to me everyone with us was paired up and all happily married. Ivy and Owen, Delia and Garrett, Marley and Gage. Even her sister Lacey, and her husband Quinn, who stopped by to say hello.

With Max right beside me in all of his tempting glory, I was fairly distracted. He radiated heat and strength. So much for my oh-so-silly idea that I had overblown him in my imagination. My body was practically on fire, and all he was doing was sitting there.

My manners kept me on autopilot as I chatted casually with the group. At some point, Max turned toward me, a beer in one hand, and the other one resting on the table. Even his hands were sexy. I knew a bit more about him than I'd known last year.

I hadn't been able to resist looking him up online. He hadn't been dishonest about what he did, but he'd left it fairly wide open and described his job as business. Business meant handling a lot of money, primarily focused on renewable energy companies. In hindsight, I couldn't help but wonder if he had known who I was at the wedding. My father was a major investor in Owen and Ivy's company, and in a number of other up-and-coming renewable resource companies.

No matter whether I thought my father was an asshole, he most certainly was not an idiot. It was doubtful that he invested for altruistic reasons. He loved to get involved in things at early stages, so he could get the biggest bang for his investment.

"So, what does 'fine' mean?" Max asked.

His expression was bland, almost inscrutable. I only hoped he couldn't read anything into mine. I knew my cheeks were flushed, and I prayed it wasn't too obvious in the dim lighting of the restaurant. I'd gotten a refill of the hard cider, needing something to take the edge off the anxiety spinning inside me.

I couldn't quite believe it, but it had been a full year since I'd had sex. Max had been my last. Lest you think I was implying that I normally had a busy sex life, you can forget that idea. No, for years, I'd been a serial monogamist. At least monogamous on my side.

Max, or rather that one night with Max, had knocked me so off-balance that for once, I hadn't gone searching for the next man to have a one-sided wishful relationship with.

When Max arched a brow, I realized my silence in response to his question might have been too long. "Fine means pretty good, I suppose. How are you?"

"Busy." He paused to take a pull from his beer, twirling the bottle between his thumb and forefinger when he set it back on the table. All I could think was that his fingers were buried inside me during a night that had been nothing but a blur of pleasure. "So tell me, how do you like being a fire-fighter?"

His question startled me, if only because he'd actually remembered that was what I said I was going to do. Thanks to my online sleuthing, I was aware of a few high-profile functions Max had attended in San Francisco—fundraisers, museum openings, and the like—always with a beautiful woman on his arm. I'd largely convinced myself that he must have forgotten me entirely. I was quite certain that Max hadn't gone without sex in the past year, yet it still surprised me that he remembered any details from our conversations.

I took a gulp of my cider and leveled my gaze with his, calling on all of my composure. It was quite necessary because having him this close, looking into his icy blue eyes and seeing the tilt of his mouth, all I wanted was to kiss him. Max made me feel wild, more forward than I usually was.

I realized my pause had *again* been too long for polite conversation when he cocked his head to the side. "You did say you had finished training, didn't you?"

"I did," I replied, nodding my head rapidly. "I like it." I paused, taking a breath. "Actually, I love it. I took a position on a crew up in Willow Brook, a few hours north of here."

"That's not far outside of Anchorage, correct?"

Nodding again, I took another sip of cider.

"I'll actually be in Anchorage for a bit soon."

"Oh? Whatever for?"

Max smiled ruefully. "Owen and I are buying out a company there. I've got a lot of cleanup to do. Perhaps we can get dinner sometime."

I stared at Max, my thoughts whirring through my mind. Max was going to be in Anchorage? So much for my idea that I would never see him again. But then, I'd already come here this weekend, knowing he would likely be here. My reckless curiosity to see him had overridden all common sense.

Max arched a brow, a gleam entering his eyes. "No dinner?"

With my rational brain practically screaming no, my wishful brain—that part of me that ran over my common sense, time and time again—was much louder and emphatic.

Yes. Hell yes. Dinner with Max? That might just be another night of heaven.

I was nodding my head before my thoughts kicked in. Max's mouth kicked up at the corner in a teasing grin. My belly spun into a series of flips and heat slid through my veins.

"Is that a yes, you mean no? Or yes to dinner?" he asked.

I nodded and then shook my head, cementing my wacky image. I felt the flash heating my cheeks and then laughed. I was terrible at this. Shrugging sheepishly, I replied, "That was a yes to dinner."

My voice came out breathy, and I mentally berated myself. This was a bad idea. I didn't need to be agreeing to have dinner with a man who had held sway in my fantasies for over a year, all because of one single night.

What little I had gathered from Ivy about Max was that she considered him a nice guy, and a guy who didn't get serious with anyone. She claimed not to know why, but she was positive someone had broken his heart and made him close off.

I'd spun that little bit of information into a man who could love someone only if it was the right person. That was another terrible habit of mine. Falling for a man who wasn't emotionally available and didn't intend to be. I convinced myself, somewhere deep down inside, underneath it all, the man in question would fall for me.

Max's blue eyes darkened. "Yes to dinner then. Now tell me, what do you think about being a firefighter?"

His entire focus was on me. It was intense and made me want to squirm. After gulping some cider, I took a breath, wishing my pulse would slow down. It was all but galloping.

"I love it. I needed a change of pace."

"From what?"

I surprised myself by answering honestly, but then, I figured it wasn't as if he couldn't get the answers from Ivy. "Well, my father runs a business, mostly investments. He wanted me to take it over, and I'm not interested. Not at all."

"I suppose I should tell you that I know your father."

This shouldn't have surprised me. Not with what I had learned about Max since our night together. His business circles most likely bumped into my father's, especially given his connections with Owen.

"Oh," I managed. I wondered if Max knew before he even met me. "How long have you known him?"

Max took a pull from his beer. "A while. I met him through Owen. If I were more polite, I would say he's a nice guy. But I'm not that polite. I happen to think he's an asshole. Even though, I'm surprised the money wasn't a lure for you," he said bluntly.

I laughed aloud, startled at Max's bluntness and somehow delighted by it as well. Most people played nice when it came to my father. He invested worldwide in many fields, and usually people wanted to stay on his good side. It was a breath of fresh air to have Max simply not give a shit.

Max shrugged at my laugh. "I'll take it as a win that I didn't offend you."

"Not at all. My father *is* an asshole. Perhaps I would've wanted to take over the company, if he hadn't been so awful to work with. Combining his asshole factor with the fact that I have no interest in investments just made it easier for me to cut ties."

"How does your father feel about you being a firefighter?"

Sadness washed through me because even if the decision felt good, I felt alone in the world. Granted, I'd felt alone long before I made this decision, but my father now ignored me more fully than he ever had before.

"He doesn't like it," I finally said. "We haven't spoken in about six months. But, it's not like we had a great relationship before that. If you know my father, you know that he likes to throw his weight around. When he doesn't get what he wants, he's a jerk."

I reached for another sip of cider only to discover it was empty. That was probably a good thing; I didn't need to get any more tipsy than I already was. I didn't need to be emotional, on top of needy, *on top* of lusting after Max.

"So tell me, Max," Ivy began from where she sat at an angle across from us, conveniently interrupting our conversation, "how long do you plan to stay in Anchorage?"

Max smoothly shifted gears, glancing over to her and smiling. "At least a month. Perhaps longer. It depends on how things look." His gaze shifted to Owen, and he shook his head slowly. "I get to do the messy part of this purchase —scouring their finances to see how much of a mess we need to clean up. Meanwhile, you and Owen will do the fun part ... dig through all the patents and take what you want."

Ivy laughed, shaking her head. "That's not so much fun either. Sometimes things get icky when this happens. But we're offering to keep on their engineers, right?" she asked, glancing from Owen to Max.

Owen's arm was resting around her shoulders, and he leaned over to press a kiss to her temple. "Of course."

Chapter Eleven

MAX

The scent of Harlow wrapped itself around me. I was experiencing another first with her. I couldn't say if I'd ever recalled the scent of a woman before. Yet, I knew Harlow's by memory. If I hadn't seen her tonight, but I'd gotten close enough, I would've known she was there by scent alone. She smelled like honey and vanilla with a hint of musk. For fuck's sake, this woman had me by the balls and she didn't even know it.

I could've asked who might be here tonight, and then I'd have been prepared to face Harlow. I'd been trying so damn hard to compartmentalize in my mind, to tell myself I'd exaggerated the effect she had on me, that I hadn't done any reconnaissance.

There was that, and the fact that I'd mentally scoffed at myself for even considering trying to find out if she'd be here. I didn't let women affect me like this. It had never been a problem for me. All Harlow had to do was simply exist on the same plane, space, and time with me, and I was caught in a riptide of lust, need, and something else.

You suggested she meet you for dinner. Are you out of your fucking mind?

The answer to that question was a definitive yes. But the effect Harlow had on me was so profound I didn't give a damn. In fact, just now, I was considering that I wanted to spend the night with her. *Tonight.* Deductive reasoning brought me to the conclusion that she was likely staying here at the lodge.

I didn't come to Diamond Creek often. My life was too busy for jaunts up to Alaska. *That's something you need to change.* So true, and I knew it.

I shook those thoughts away because I didn't need to dwell on my internal restlessness. The compass kept spinning without a clear direction, even when I willfully forced myself in one. Losing myself in Harlow was such a temptation, I couldn't *not* consider it. And yet, hundreds of warning sirens were going off at full blast in my mind at the idea.

I was normally a rational man, and yet, my intellect was no match for the fire Harlow set ablaze inside me. I could feel the heat of her body, from where I sat next to her. My cock was hard, pressing against my zipper.

Control wasn't usually an issue for me. In fact, even though I'd once had a woman stomp all over my heart, when it came to sex, I'd always been in control. That was saying something, considering I'd been young the last time any woman affected me like this. For men—at least from my experience—the years of adolescence and the early years of adulthood were mostly dictated by one's cock.

Harlow's hair was down, its dark glossy sheen glinting under the dim lighting in the restaurant. Her wide eyes reminded me of chocolate and espresso, two pleasures I happened to love. Yet, they didn't hold a candle to looking into her gaze. Her eyes were so expressive. I hadn't forgotten seeing her walls fall when she let go.

Her shields were up now, her gaze guarded, with only hints of vulnerability flickering in her eyes. Unlike at the wedding, when she'd been wearing that slip of a dress, tonight she wore a fitted cotton shirt of rich blue. It dipped down in a V, conveniently offering me teasing glimpses of the shadowed valley between her breasts. She'd paired her shirt with jeans and cowboy boots. When she stood to walk to the restroom a few minutes ago, all I could envision were those cowboy boots on her bare legs as she wrapped them around my waist.

Owen said something to me, dragging my attention away from Harlow. This was definitely not the place to let my thoughts get lost in her, not surrounded by a group as we were. If I were being honest with myself, it was impossible for me to be near Harlow and not have half of my attention on her. But, I was a gentleman and managed to shift enough attention to Owen. Within minutes, I was deep into a conversation with him about our latest acquisition. We'd met in Anchorage for a mere two days to finalize our purchase. I was here at the lodge for the weekend, and then I'd be heading back up to the company we now owned.

The next few weeks would be tense; they always were. The offices were filled with people who worked for the previous owners, and this could make for some tense interactions. We owned everything now, down to the paper clips in the trays on their desks. Owen always volunteered his time during this phase, but I knew he hated it.

Not that I liked it. Yet, I supposed I was more dispassionate about it than him. I tried to keep it in the back of my mind that we were good bosses, that even if people there were loyal to their former owners, they had to learn that their jobs had been at risk by virtue of the poor decisions made. We didn't bash anyone. That wasn't how we approached these situations. Under the best of circumstances, it would be an awkward few weeks. The idea of being within casting distance of Harlow during those weeks made it quite appealing.

It got late, and the group started to break apart. Harlow

stood to give Ivy a hug good night before Ivy rounded the table to drop a kiss on my cheek. "Thanks for coming, Max. It was good to see you," she said.

"Of course. It was great catching up."

Somehow, Harlow slipped away when I wasn't paying attention. At the last moment, I saw the swing of her hair as she turned through the archway near the reception area.

I hastily snagged my jacket and followed her, relieved the social niceties were over. If you had told me I would be chasing a woman through a ski lodge simply because I wanted her, I would have told you that was fucking insane. And yet, that was exactly what I was doing. My stride was long, and I was through the reception area in a flash, catching sight of Harlow's dark hair and her gorgeous backside. I hadn't forgotten the way those silky locks felt wrapped around my hand as I buried myself deep inside her from behind.

We'd gotten our mileage out of that single night. I was fairly certain I'd taken her at least three times, if not more. I was usually a man of precision, yet that night had been nothing but a blur of raw, hot lust and pleasure.

It was also the only night where I stayed in the same bed after sex. I usually took care of matters and then left. But when time lost all meaning, well, I supposed things were different then.

Rounding the corner into the elevator lobby, I found Harlow staring out the windows facing over the mountains. There was already a decent amount of snow on the peaks, even though it was only late November. A half moon was rising behind the mountains, its silvery light cast across the silhouette of the mountains dark against the sky.

I walked to her side. "Harlow."

She jumped a little when I spoke her name, her breath drawing in sharply. Her espresso gaze swung to mine, a flush cresting on her cheeks. For fuck's sake. I was used to feeling balanced; frankly, to feeling as though I had the power in most situations.

I wasn't *that* guy. One of those assholes who needed to swing his weight around, metaphorically swinging his dick around. No, rather, I enjoyed being able to call the shots in my life. It grated at me slightly that Harlow illuminated how much I took for granted. Especially when it came to women. I wasn't accustomed to calculating, but with her, everything was a calculation. Because I wanted her that much. Something shimmered under the surface of my raw desire, driving me closer, throwing me off-balance.

We simply stared at each other for a few beats. An elevator reached the ground floor, the distinct pinging sound echoing across the tiled space. Harlow spun around quickly, striding for the elevator as the doors slid open with a soft *whoosh*. I followed her. There wasn't even a question about that.

Once we were in the elevator, she glanced to me. "Which floor?"

I had already noticed that we were on the same floor. "Three."

The number three glowed soft blue from where she had already pressed it. She stepped back, one hand curling around the railing that ran around the elevator, the other reaching up to twirl a lock of her glossy hair around her finger.

My brain fuzzed offline. I was stepping closer to Harlow before I calculated how it might be interpreted. When I was right beside her, the sweet hint of vanilla drifted to me and I could see the flutter of her pulse in her neck, and my entire body tightened, need flashing through me.

With the depth of my attraction to her, I had been in bad enough shape as it was. It was all made worse by the fact that I knew precisely how it felt to be with her. I knew the silky soft feel of her skin, the clench of her channel around me, and how wild she was. For a woman as guarded and controlled as she came across, when the walls fell, it was as if everything she'd been holding back poured out.

She never looked away from me, and I saw the flicker of something in her gaze. I didn't know what the hell it was about her eyes, but they had a straight line to my heart, which wasn't something I thought about much. With nothing more than a heated look from Harlow, it thumped erratically. All the while, I was driven to her, unable to step back. I took another step closer, lifting my hand and catching that lock of hair sliding in a circle around her finger. Curling my hand around hers, I moved closer, savoring the hitch in her breath.

There were mere inches separating us. She took a breath, and her breasts pressed against me. Her pulse fluttered wildly and her flush deepened.

"We had ground rules," she whispered.

For a beat, I was confused about what she meant, and then I remembered. "Ah, we did. Refresh my memory."

I could sense her trying to batten down the hatches, to pull herself in. She didn't push me away, so I took that as a win.

"We said just once. There would be no expectations if we saw each other again."

My memory sharpened. "True. I don't have any expectations. I just want you. Is that breaking a rule?"

I was genuinely curious. Even though it would take most of my discipline, if she told me to back the hell off, I would.

Harlow simply stared at me, her eyes widening. I could practically see the gears shifting in her brain. She waited so long to answer, the sound of her voice was a featherlight lash to the lust twisting inside of me when she spoke.

"No. I suppose it's not. I just..." Her words trailed off as she cocked her head to the side.

I slid my hand down her forearm, resting it along the dip in her waist. The waiting was killing me. Because I wanted to kiss her. Fiercely.

"I don't know if this is a good idea," she finally confessed.

She was damn right. It was a terrible idea. I was already tangled up in her, the force of my need almost binding me to her.

There I was, a man who eschewed emotional attachments, carrying on a conversation that was all kinds of emotionally loaded. "What are you worried about?"

We couldn't have been in the elevator that long when I realized we had already come to a stop on our floor. The door whispered open, and the sound of voices down the hall nudged me out of my half trance.

Without thinking, I was curling my hand around hers and turning. I simply expected her to follow me. Initially she did, but then she stopped, giving my hand a little tug. We were alone in the hallway now; the group of guests that had passed us by were stepping into the elevator behind us.

"What?" I asked.

"I don't know if this is a good idea," she repeated.

"I know. I just want to get somewhere private to talk."

She must not have been expecting that because she laughed. "Um, okay. This is my room," she said, gesturing to the door beside her.

Once we were inside, she walked to the windows. Her shoulders were tense, and she hugged her arms around her waist, looking out at the mountains in the darkness. The soft glow of the moon was cast across part of the view. The rest was blanketed in shadow from the tall trees along the slopes.

"So tell me why this isn't a good idea."

I stopped beside her, feeling the tension emanating from her. She was practically vibrating. She turned to face me, and the pain I saw in her eyes was like a knife slicing across the surface of my heart. I didn't know who had hurt her, but I would gladly kill them on her behalf.

I almost laughed aloud as my feelings screamed out their thoughts. I was usually a rational man, certainly not one prone to emotional decisions. Chasing after an unknown person who may or may not have hurt Harlow most definitely fell into that category.

She tore her gaze free and gave her head a shake. "It doesn't really matter. I just want to kiss you once more," she said, surprising the hell out of me.

I didn't know if I could handle just a kiss. But you might as well have dragged me through hell before I stopped myself. In a flash, she was stepping to me, sliding her hand up around my nape and arching into me as I bent to meet her. The moment her lips touched mine, hot electricity jolted me like lightning to my system. I didn't know what she meant this kiss to be, but inside of a hot second, her tongue was tangling with mine and my hand was sliding down her spine to cup her sweet ass. She fit against me perfectly, just tall enough that my cock nestled at the apex of her thighs, and her breasts pressed into my chest.

Jesus fucking Christ. This woman set me on fire. I was hard as a rock and so hot for her I could hardly breathe. I dove into the warm sweetness of her mouth, loving how she matched me, stroke for stroke, nip for nip. She kissed wildly, throwing herself into it the moment it started.

Just as quickly, she broke free, stumbling back. "See," she stated, on the heels of a gasp, "that's why this is a bad idea. You make me crazy. I have a terrible habit of falling for men who ultimately don't want anything."

I wanted to ask her what she meant. But when she looked at me, and I saw the tears glistening in her eyes, I had a desire to tug her into my arms and shield her from the world, which was crazy.

"Harlow..." I started to say.

She cut me off. "Please, Max. I'm sure I'll see you again, but if you don't leave now, I'll do something stupid. I really don't want to do that."

I wanted to beg her to do something stupid. I didn't think she could be any more reckless than me. When it came to Harlow, reckless, crazy, wild desire stole my thoughts, took over my body, and made my heart want things I'd thought long forgotten.

But I didn't beg. Somehow—hell if I knew how—I sensed I shouldn't push. I could almost see her metaphorically pulling her dignity around her shoulders and holding it tight. I turned and walked to the door. She was polite and followed me over, standing there quietly.

"This isn't over, Harlow," I said as I looked down into her eyes.

Bending low, I pressed a kiss to her lips, bracing myself to withstand the lightning bolt of contact with her.

Returning to my suite down the hall, I took a cold shower, made do with a mechanical release, and fell into a restless night of sleep, wondering why the hell I didn't want to run from Harlow.

Chapter Twelve

HARLOW

The following morning, I woke in my bed at Last Frontier Lodge. Alone. My mind spun back to the night before, when I kissed Max and then came to my senses. Simply recalling the kiss had my lips tingling and butterflies spinning in my belly. The depth of my attraction to Max was intense, and ran deep as a river inside of me. I couldn't quite believe I'd managed to break away to tell him the plain truth—it was a bad idea.

Tears pricked hot at the backs of my eyes. Annoyed with myself, I kicked back the covers and headed for the shower. I wasn't on the verge of tears over Max. Rather, that well of emotion stemmed from regret over my trail of bad choices in men. Not that there had been that many, yet each and every one had been a repeat performance of me wishfully, desperately, hoping for something that wasn't there.

The last thing I needed to do was hand my silly, foolish heart over to a man who I quite clearly knew didn't want anything close to what I did. I kept recalling the gentle prodding of my last therapist, the one I'd gone to see after my miscarriage.

I'd been a bit of an emotional disaster at the time. My thoughts spun back.

Skidding sideways inside, unable to pull myself out of the slide, out of the emotional wreck I'd created within myself, I sat staring at my therapist. Her brown eyes were soft, but hard to read.

"Harlow, I know you want to find someone. That's what many people want. But perhaps you need to stop looking for love in the way you have. To remember that no one can replace what you lost when your mother died and your father went on to treat you as an afterthought."

She went on to say all this stuff about recapitulation, which was something about re-creating the same dynamic that I had with my father, time and again. I lost track of the details, but the concept rang a bell inside.

"You think that's what I'm doing?" I asked with a sniffle. I was crying. Again.

At her slow nod, I managed to take a deep breath. Oddly, it was calming to gain some perspective on the painful pattern in my relationships, or lack thereof.

It was a bit of a miracle I'd somehow been able to instill some of her observations. I hadn't had a train wreck of a relationship since then. Then again, I hadn't had a relationship at all. I'd had a whopping total of a single one-night stand—the most intense sex *ever* in my life.

As I showered, the steam washing away the stinging pain in my heart, I actually felt a little proud of myself. I'd set a boundary for my emotional sanity and held to it. While I dressed, my thoughts poked at the sore spots in my heart. Max wasn't an asshole. Even if I hadn't known him via his long-term friendship with Owen, I sensed it. I knew from his own words last year, when I had set the ground rules that I needed for my own sanity, that he wasn't looking for a relationship. He'd said as much. I needed to trust that he meant it and not hope for more.

Plus, I knew from what little I'd let myself look up online

that he didn't do serious relationships. He appeared to have nothing more than casual dates with women who were perfectly happy to be seen with him for a bit of social glitter.

I wouldn't fit that bill. Not at all.

———

A while later, I made my way downstairs for an early breakfast in the lodge restaurant. I was quietly minding my own business, enjoying my coffee and a delicious omelet, when I felt Max's presence before I even saw him. The hair lifted on the back of my neck, and a prickle ran down my spine, heat radiating through me.

He was there before I even turned around to see him approaching. He stood by the table, glancing down at me. His black hair was damp and his blue eyes bright. The strong, clean lines of his features were gorgeous. It wasn't quite fair for a man to be as beautiful as Max Channing was. He exuded quiet confidence, strength, and elemental masculinity. There was nothing feminine about him. Sweet hell, I could look at him all day.

That was dangerous.

"Can I join you?" he asked.

I knew I should say no, yet I didn't want to. I wanted him to sit down with me, have breakfast, then drag him upstairs to my room and take a few hours to get lost in him and the desire beating like a drum between us.

Crazy—I was that fucking crazy.

Just as I was stealing myself to hold the line, Delia appeared beside us, casting a smile between us. "Good morning, you two. Max, I think I should get you some coffee. If I recall, you like it black," she said warmly.

"You recall correctly," he replied, his mouth hitching up at the corner and promptly sending my belly into a quick flip.

It felt as if my hormones were doing a performance for him, a little dance, to let *his* hormones know just how happy they were to see him.

Now, it would be rude if I didn't let Max join me, considering Delia presumed we were eating together; a natural guess, given our shared friends. I had just started to dig into my omelet, and it was quite obvious I wasn't finished with breakfast.

"I'll be right back with your coffee, and I'll get you a refill," Delia said, her eyes flicking to my half-empty coffee cup.

"That would be great, thanks," I managed.

Max was polite enough not to sit down yet, but it didn't really matter. I gestured to the chair across for me. "Go ahead, have a seat."

Max's mouth hitched at the corner again, and I almost laughed aloud. All the man had to do was smile and my nipples perked up as if to greet him.

The moment he sat down, I became acutely aware of how small the table was. I was seated at one of the square tables beside the windows. One end of the dining area in the lodge had large round tables and booths, while the other had scattered small tables. This table was, at best, two feet square.

Max's knee bumped one of mine when he slid his chair forward, the brief point of contact sending a zing of electricity through my system. I decided right then and there that I would have to cut my weekend short. Max was way too tempting.

"How are you this morning?" he asked.

I took a fortifying gulp of my coffee and nodded. "I'm well, and yourself?"

He cocked his head to the side, glancing out the windows at the ridiculously stunning view of the mountains, with the sun just rising above them. His eyes cut back to me, immediately holding my gaze. Even though I hadn't spent much time with Max, I was becoming accustomed to the fact that whenever he looked at me, it felt as though we were alone in the world.

"I'm well," he finally said. "I've been thinking..." He paused when Delia came into view, crossing the restaurant with a tray and aiming straight for our table.

"Here you go." She set a coffee on the table for Max and quickly refilled mine. "I'm guessing you'd like something to eat," she said, her gaze flicking to him.

"Of course I do. I'll take whatever you recommend."

"Harlow is having our special this morning—a smoked salmon omelet with cream cheese and green onions."

"I'll take the same," he said smoothly.

With a wink, she spun away, weaving her way through the restaurant and checking on a few other tables. I was kind of hoping Max had forgotten whatever he'd been about to say. Although, I was terribly curious to know what he'd been thinking about.

He hadn't forgotten. The moment his icy blue gaze locked with mine, he picked up right where he left off. "So, as I was saying, I've been thinking. I'm not sure why you think this is such a bad idea, but I think it would be foolish not to see what happens."

Though he didn't specify, I knew precisely what *this* was. He was speaking to the wild, crazy, thrumming desire between us. I didn't quite know what he meant beyond that.

"I'm not sure I understand."

He reached across the table, trailing his index finger across my knuckles, and my grip tightened around my coffee cup. His touch was a blaze of fire across my skin. My pulse lunged, and my heart started knocking against my ribs.

"You said this was a bad idea. I'm not sure you'll tell me why, but I have a guess," he countered.

"What's that?"

"I think perhaps, you think I only want sex."

No, because I'm all fucked up inside my head and can't get out of my own way.

I ordered my inner monologue to shut up. It was quiet for a few beats, and I felt held within the intensity of his gaze. Even though my body was flat-out acting crazy, somehow the look in his eyes comforted me. And that was even crazier.

When I didn't say anything, he continued, "I won't lie. I definitely want you, but I know the way we are together isn't something that comes along every day. I propose we forget those ground rules and just see what happens."

His finger trailed across my knuckles again. I couldn't have looked away from his eyes if I tried. It was like being locked in by a tractor beam. Not that I knew what that felt like, but I'd seen my share of outer space television shows and movies.

Taking a shaky breath, I was relieved when he dropped his hand away to take a sip of coffee.

I surprised myself by speaking honestly. "It's not that I don't want you, but I tend to expect too much from men. I don't have a great track record, and I'm guessing casual is the name of the game for you. I don't do casual well."

Max never once looked away, his eyes narrowing slightly at my last comment. I sensed he was considering his words carefully.

"I was in love once," he said abruptly, startling the hell out of me.

"Huh?" was my brilliant reply.

His low chuckle sent a shiver chasing over my skin. "Yes, I was in love once. Things didn't end well. I suppose my point is that I understand being careful."

"Careful?" I didn't know why he was telling me this. It was so surprising, it knocked me off-balance.

I wasn't quite ready to delve further and was relieved when Delia reappeared and headed toward our table. She served Max's omelet, topped off our coffees, and chatted for a few minutes. While she was there, Marley Hamilton came out. She worked at the lodge alongside her husband Gage, and they lived upstairs in private quarters. She had her cherubic toddler Holly in her arms, who had pink cheeks, wide mossy green eyes, and the same auburn hair as her mother. She was utterly adorable.

My heartbeat stuttered, reminding me that there was the kind of careful Max was perhaps referring to, and the kind of careful I needed to keep from getting hurt again. While Marley was chatting with us, I practically shoveled the rest of my omelet in my mouth, managing to stand and get ready to leave as soon as I was done.

I didn't care if I was running. I was going to take this moment to say my goodbyes. I didn't know where Max intended to go with this conversation, but I already knew I was barreling down a path with which I was far too familiar.

The chemistry I felt with Max was powerful, and the intimacy threading into it terrified me because I knew I would get hurt. I'd been envisioning a picket fence and two-point-five kids since I was a little girl, with any man that might serve as a stand-in. I certainly didn't need to be doing that with a man I wanted as fiercely as Max. Because when the inevitable happened, I would then be facing the layered complication of our shared friendship with Owen and Ivy.

Marley looked to me as I stood, her smile warm. "So, how long are you staying?"

"Actually, I have to head back today for work tomorrow," I lied. I'd been intending to stay all weekend. With Max down the hallway, that was a disastrous plan. "It was great to see you."

Marley surprised me by tugging me into a quick hug, with Holly getting squished between us and catching hold of my hair as Marley stepped back. She giggled when I freed it.

I looked down to Max, ordering my cheeks not to flush. "It was good to see you too," I said, studiously keeping my

expression bland. His eyes coasted over me. I didn't know
how to interpret his expression, yet I sensed he was far too
perceptive.

"And you. I'll give you a call from Anchorage," he finally
said.

Chapter Thirteen

HARLOW

Three days later, I was still wondering if Max even had my phone number.

I finally decided to fess up and tell Ivy about Max. She'd just called to check in and told me she thought I was lying when I left early. I *had* been lying. I felt bad about it, so I told her the plain truth.

"Ivy, I can't deal with Max."

"What do you mean? Max is a really nice guy."

I bit my lip and took a deep breath as I leaned back into the cushions on my couch. I rented a small house on a pretty little lot not too far outside of downtown Willow Brook. Susannah offered it to me when she moved in with her now-husband, Ward. It was a cute A-frame cabin with decks on both floors. The downstairs living room area was bright and light-filled, with windows stretching from floor to ceiling in the front wall and offering a view of a field and Swan Lake in the distance. The kitchen was behind the living room with a bathroom and laundry off to the side. A loft with two bedrooms and a bathroom comprised the upstairs.

I had returned home after breakfast at the lodge, never

giving Max an opportunity to finish that conversation with me, and not even finding time to say goodbye to Ivy and Owen. I'd been rather busy telling myself in the two days that followed that leaving had *absolutely* been the smart move.

It had taken me two years not to stumble into another bad choice, and I was holding firm against the biggest temptation I'd ever faced. No matter what Max had meant to say, I seriously doubted he was going to tell me he was madly in love with me.

I'd worked too damn hard to establish a healthy sense of self and to learn to stop searching high and low for the love my father never gave me. Despite the temptation that was Max, and despite the fact I had shored myself up inside, I still worried I was too vulnerable. With Max, I felt as if I were standing on the precipice of something, a test of sorts.

Because, you see, I didn't quite know how to do this part of it. Not that I thought Max was a good candidate for it, but I didn't know how to let myself be vulnerable. I'd done it wrong forever and now I didn't know how to do it in a healthy way.

I could practically sense Ivy's worry vibrating through the cell phone line. "I think I'm missing something. Did something happen with you and Max?"

On the heels of a fortifying breath, I told her the truth. "Yes. You know how you said you were kind of trying to throw us together at your place?"

"Uh huh, but you told me that Max didn't stay, that he left for business."

"I wasn't lying about that. I might have neglected to mention that he stayed for one night before he left. I might've also neglected to mention that we had crazy hot sex."

Even saying it out loud made my cheeks hot.

"*What*?! How could you not tell me this?"

"Because it was an epically bad idea. You know I've been

trying not to be stupid about men anymore. Max is not exactly available for a relationship. You know it, and I know it."

Ivy was quiet and I could practically feel the wheels spinning in her mind. After a moment, she sighed. "I think he could be."

"Right, and I specialize in wanting things that could maybe work out and never do. Ivy, you know I can't deal with another train wreck of my own making. I'd rather be celibate for the rest of my life than end up in yet *another* relationship that isn't really a relationship. Plus, he's your friend and Owen's friend. I don't want to get my hopes up and then have it fizzle, and *then* have it be all awkward if we ever run into each other."

"Ugh, did he hurt your feelings already? I'll kick his ass," Ivy declared, the good friend that she was.

"No, God no. It wasn't like that. It was just... Well, let's just say there's some chemistry there. It was just one night. I didn't make any promises, and neither did he. I need to keep it like that. So to keep from doing something stupid, I left."

"I wish you would stop completely shutting out men," Ivy muttered.

"It's better than getting my heart stomped on again and again."

"Max is not going to stomp on anyone's heart," she insisted.

I sighed, knowing Ivy meant well. "Look, it's cute that you want to set us up, but you know as well as I do that it's not smart for me to try anything casual. You've told me yourself Max doesn't get serious."

Her sigh filtered through the phone. "I know, but there was a reason I tried to throw you two together. Obviously, I was totally right about the chemistry."

"So you were, but I need to take care of myself."

"I hate that you're sequestering yourself like this. This isn't just about Max. You don't give *anybody* a chance."

"I give plenty of people chances. I just don't have good luck when it comes to men. Trust me, there's no shortage of chemistry with Max. But I can already feel myself doing what I usually do. I would fall for him and that's just dumb. He's got plenty of gorgeous women more than willing to be an arm ornament for him. Plus, I live here and he lives in San Francisco."

"You know, I don't think you're being fair to Max. It's not like he's a player. Honestly, I'm not sure what happened but he treats dating like business. He's a really nice guy, and I think you two could have a shot together. Don't throw geography in my face either. He's even talked to Owen about getting out of the city."

I *so* wanted to believe what she was selling, but my heart was too fragile, and falling for Max was a recipe for disaster.

"Ivy—"

She cut me right off. "No, I'm serious. I'm not being a ridiculous romantic. Owen thinks Max likes you. I wasn't going to say anything because I didn't know you had *sex* with him," she said, emphasizing her words. I knew she wouldn't like it that I'd kept it from her, but this very conversation was what I had been trying to avoid. "Seriously, it's not healthy for you to avoid men forever. I know you went to therapy, and that you're working on not constantly searching for someone to sweep you off your feet, but you have to give someone a chance at some point, if you want a shot at a relationship."

My throat felt tight. I tucked my feet in the gap between the couch cushions, tugging the blanket over my knees a little tighter. "I know. I'm just trying to figure out when."

"Well, I'm going to do some digging on Max to find out why he's never serious. I know he wouldn't treat you like shit. He's not an asshole."

"I know he's not an asshole."

I could practically feel her eye roll through the phone.

"Anyway, on a lighter note, how was the night?" Ivy asked, her sly tone clear as a bell through the phone line.

My cheeks got hot all over again. Ivy wasn't even here to see me, but thinking about that night with Max was, um, hot and bothersome. "It was memorable," I said.

Ivy laughed. "I bet it was."

"There, I hope you're satisfied now. Look, I gotta go. It's getting late, and I need to go into Anchorage tomorrow to take care of some errands."

"Okay, okay. I'll report back as soon as I get more info from Owen. Whether you want it or not, I think Max might be good for you."

I groaned.

Ivy laughed. "Love you, girl."

"Ditto, talk to you soon."

Tossing the phone on the coffee table, I leaned my head back on the couch, staring up at the ceiling.

The ceiling in this house was great for staring. It was white pine and offered a variety of pretty knots to count. I idly counted them as I considered my conversation with Ivy. Though I knew steering clear of Max was the smart choice, the problem was I *so* desperately wanted to give *anything* with Max a chance.

Sex with him was so amazing, maybe it would be worth the heartbreak.

With a muttered curse, I kicked the blanket off my legs and stood to go make some hot chocolate. I looked out the kitchen windows while I waited for the water to boil. Snow was falling lightly, the flakes glittering like fairy dust from the sky, with the lights on the back deck illuminating them.

In the time I'd been here, I'd grown to love the seasons. I'd also grown to love being in one place. I wasn't sure if it was because my mother died when I was so young, or because of my father's benign neglect of me growing up, but I'd spent most of my life carrying a ball of tension inside, always worrying about what might happen next and never really knowing. As an adult, I could understand that my father probably had his schedule lined out a full year in advance. But, as a little girl, all I'd known was I bounced from one place to the other.

I sipped my hot chocolate and considered my childhood. The most time I'd spent anywhere for a stretch was in North Carolina. Before my mother died out of the blue from a brain aneurysm, that was where we lived in between my father's travel. I'd only been six years old when she died, so my memories weren't too sharp, but the clearest childhood memories I had were of times with her. My mother's family was also in North Carolina, so I occasionally spent summers with them as I grew up. It was always scorching hot and humid, but I loved it. I wasn't too close to her family, but they were the closest thing to family I had. They sent me Christmas cards and gave me gifts, and always hugged me when they saw me.

My mother's death eroded what little stability I'd had in my life before that. Being here in Willow Brook, in this small town on the edge of the wilderness, where I'd been staying in the same cute cabin for almost a year, was a blessing. I loved it. I loved my job, and I loved the friends that I was slowly making.

It was a little lonely sometimes, but I would take lonely over the knot of tension I'd carried inside for so long.

As usual, my thoughts drifted to Max, and I fell asleep with him on my mind.

————

The following morning, as planned, I hopped in my little truck and drove to Anchorage. My father cut me off from any money through him, but I had funds saved up from a trust my mother had set side. I'd used a little bit of it to buy myself a nice truck and get situated out here. The rest would wait.

The wind was gusting, and the air was icy cold this late November day as I drove east toward Anchorage. I loved winter mornings here, with the sky stained purple and the snow bright on the mountains.

I hit up a few department stores once I got to town. Beyond getting some things for myself, I had a rather lengthy list of items to pick up for friends and acquaintances in Willow Brook. I'd learned early on here that if you were taking a trip to Anchorage, it was common to serve as a delivery person. Janet needed some supplies for the bakery, while Ward had asked me to pick up an engine block, of all things. He had assured me the guys at the mechanic shop would load it into the back of my truck for me, and he would help unload it on the other end with some of the guys at the station.

By the time late afternoon rolled around, the bed of my truck was packed and the weather was getting bad. Fast. The days were short this time of year, and we were only weeks away from the shortest day of the year.

Nothing I had was perishable, so I decided not to hedge my bets, and stay the night in a hotel. Because I'd stayed in a gazillion hotels over the years, I had quite a few points racked up, so I headed straight for one of the chains where I had plenty. It was conveniently a luxury place, which was comforting when the wind and snow were howling outside. After I checked in, I chatted with Ivy for a few minutes when she called.

"Well, since you're in Anchorage, maybe you should actually, you know, try to meet someone," Ivy said, her sly tone evident through the phone line.

"Seriously?" I countered, shaking my head, even though she wasn't here to see me.

"The only way to meet someone is to *meet* them somehow," she said with a laugh before we said our goodbyes.

Although it wasn't for that reason, or so I told myself, I decided to stop by the bar and enjoy a nightcap.

Settled at the bar in the corner, I was enjoying a glass of warm, mulled wine when a man came and sat beside me. I silently swore. I'd wanted peace and quiet tonight, not to get picked up.

I forced myself to actually look at the man because Ivy was always giving me crap for not even trying, and pointing out I would never find someone if I refused to pay attention. But this man didn't even ping in my system. He was handsome enough, objectively speaking. He had dark brown hair, with eyes to match, and looked to be a businessman based on the way he was dressed.

"Can I get you a drink?" he asked by way of greeting.

I lifted the more than halfway full glass I had in my hand. "No thanks, I'm all set."

"So what brings you here?"

"Oh, just a few errands."

I was trying to not be rude, but not be particularly welcoming either. He didn't take the hint when I glanced away to the television above the bar.

"I guess it's my lucky night."

I smiled tightly and saw the bartender cast her eyes my way. There were plenty of other places for this man to sit. I didn't know what she read in my expression, but she casually made her way over to our end of the bar.

"You ready for your check?" she asked, her gaze on me.

Part of me wanted to say yes, but I was kind of pissed. I had just wanted to relax and have a drink. Instead, I had some guy who wanted to hit on me, and I wanted no part of it.

Before I could reply, a voice sounded over my shoulder. "There you are!"

I knew that voice. *Max*. The mere sound instantly lifted the hairs on the back of my neck and sent a wash of heat through me.

I was also quite relieved he happened to be here. That was the thing about him. The risk to my heart was steep, but he was a good man, and I doubted he would approach a woman the way this man had. Not that the man had even done anything wrong, per se. But I'd sent off no signals implying I was interested in anything, and yet he'd parked himself right there, with every intention of staying, and dubbed himself "lucky" for it.

"I was just looking for you in the lobby," Max continued as he reached me, actually stepping between me and the man beside me.

There wasn't much room, and Max was a large man. It was a bit awkward. I didn't mind, especially not when he slid his arm around my waist and leaned over, pressing his lips against my temple.

"She's been waiting for me, but I'm running late," he said by way of explanation to the bartender. "We'll just grab a table, if you don't mind. If you could bring a menu over, that would be even better."

Chapter Fourteen

HARLOW

Max completely ignored the man beside me, sliding his hand down my back where I sat on the barstool and exerting gentle pressure. I wasn't going to argue the point. I was in no mood to have some random guy trying to flirt with me.

There was also the blunt truth that when it came to Max, I found myself, time and time again, unable to resist the magnetic pull toward him. Within moments, I was walking with him close at my side, his hand not leaving the dip in my lower back. The heat of his touch was like a brand, filtering through the silk of my blouse and the camisole I wore underneath, all the way down to my cowboy boots.

Max led me over to a small table in the corner. He held my chair out for me, and I slipped into it. My pulse had taken off at a gallop with my heartbeat echoing through my entire body. That thrumming need only Max elicited spun through my veins. Whenever I was with him, all my senses were heightened. I could feel his heat and strength, catching a hint of his clean, crisp scent, and felt the burn of his gaze when he sat down across from me.

"Hello, Harlow," Max said, hooking an elbow across the

back of his chair as he leaned back.

"Hi, Max." That was about all I could think to say. I was too busy trying to quell my body's response to him into submission.

He was quiet for a beat, his gaze far too knowing and perceptive for my comfort. "I hope you don't mind my interruption. I happened to be staying here, and Ivy texted me that you were here," he finally said.

Oh dear God. I should've known Ivy would send Max my way. She didn't even mention he happened to be at the same hotel. But I wasn't going to get into that with Max.

"No, it was convenient, actually. I don't know who that guy was, but he seemed to think I was here for something other than just a drink."

Max's mouth stretched into a slow grin. Sweet hell. His grins sent my body skidding sideways inside. The moment he looked over at me, my panties were drenched. "Good to know my guess was on target."

Scrambling inside, I felt almost willful against the tide of need crashing through me. "What would you have done if I'd *wanted* him to flirt with me?"

I was genuinely curious, but I was also taunting him. Perhaps it was crazy, but then, just about everything I did when it came to Max was crazy.

His icy blue gaze narrowed. "I wouldn't have liked it. Not one bit," he said flatly.

The air around us felt charged, snapping and crackling with the electricity between us. A waitress arrived. I presumed the bartender had sent someone over after Max's request for the menu. She paused and smiled brightly between us. "Hi, I understand you'd like dinner."

"We would." The waitress set down menus for us, and Max glanced over at me. "Have you eaten?" he asked.

I shook my head. I'd just been planning to order at the bar.

The waitress glanced at Max. "Would you like something

to drink?" she asked, filling our waters.

"A beer would be great, whatever you have on tap, thanks." He flicked his gaze to my nearly-finished drink. "You?"

"I'm all set, thanks. Just water."

If Max had an opinion about that, he kept it to himself. The waitress hurried back to the bar for his beer, and I flipped through the menu, quickly deciding on a burger and fries.

"You don't have to buy me dinner," I said, setting the menu on the edge of the table.

He closed his menu, lifting his eyes to mine. "I'm buying you dinner."

I rolled my eyes. "It's not necessary."

"Precisely the point, so why argue?"

I didn't care to debate the issue with him, so I simply shrugged. Our waitress arrived, and we both ordered burgers and fries. After she left, I decided to stick to mundane topics.

"So, how's the acquisition going? Is this something you and Owen work on together?"

Max nodded, taking a sip of his beer. "It's not like we do this often. This is the third time we've bought up a struggling company. We only do it when it looks like the company's about to fold, and when they have patents we might want in renewable energies. He doesn't love this part, and he focuses more on design than I do. I usually handle a lot of the logistics and numbers. I don't mind. I suppose I do a better job of compartmentalizing than he does."

We moved into a rather easygoing conversation about the company they'd acquired. I knew what Ivy and Owen did, but in talking with Max, I realized he was just as involved in the field of engineering and renewable energy as they were. I probably shouldn't have been so relieved to talk about business, but I was. It kept my mind off the way my body practically spun like a top at Max's presence.

Chapter Fifteen

HARLOW

Max was, as would be expected, an intelligent, well-informed conversationalist when it came to talking business. He was clearly passionate about sustainability and focusing his energies in that area, and freely acknowledged, while he had the engineering skills, his facility with numbers, and ability to look at the long game when planning for business had shifted him into more of a management role.

Dinner passed quickly. I eschewed any further drinks, telling myself rather sternly that I needed to stay sober. I was in bad enough shape with Max as it was, I sure as hell didn't need to get tipsy and let my guard down. I'd have been perfectly happy to crawl across the table and straddle his lap. Not because I was an exhibitionist, but because he was *that* inviting.

When the waitress paused by our table, checking to see if either one of us needed a drink and to collect our now empty plates, I shook my head. Max regarded me after she walked away.

"Not that I care one way or the other, but is there a reason you don't want anything to drink?"

I surprised myself with my blunt answer. "Because I don't need to do anything else stupid with you."

For a flash, I sensed my comments stunned him. Max shuttered his eyes quickly, and I experienced a sting of regret. He was quiet for a beat, draining the last of his beer.

"You have me pegged, don't you?"

I started to shake my head, but then I shrugged. What the hell? I'd already been more blunt than was perhaps wise. "Maybe."

Max leaned forward slightly. Even that small shift in the distance between us sent my pulse even higher and fuzzed my thoughts. His blue gaze held mine. "That's not fair, Harlow."

"I didn't..." My words trailed off when I didn't even know what I meant to say.

Max reached across the table and curled his hand around mine where it rested on the table. The simple feel of his skin against mine made my heart kick against my ribs and my breath hitch.

"I'm not going to pretend I'm a saint. But I know this thing between us isn't going anywhere. I've never made promises I can't keep, but I have enough sense to know no one can promise something in advance. It would be foolish for us to ignore this."

His voice was like rough velvet, almost hypnotic. I couldn't look away, and my mind narrowed, focusing on the soft brush of his thumb across the back of my knuckles. Because that was how helpless I was, caught in a riptide of need and desire over nothing more than the barest touch from him.

I heard Ivy's voice ringing in my head, pointing out that I wasn't giving anyone a shot. Perhaps, just maybe, I could let this play out, if I walked into it with my eyes wide open for once, without hoping for more.

Max's thumb brushed across the back of my knuckles, the subtle gesture erotic. I'd never known my knuckles were that sensitive. The air was heavy around us as I tried to take a deep breath and failed. My heart was pounding too hard, and my body felt as if I'd just run a marathon. It was crazy; all I was doing was sitting there with Max's hand curled over mine and his touch teasing me.

"Okay," I finally said.

Our waitress arrived with our check just then. Max never let go of my hand, reaching into the pocket of his jeans and tugging his wallet out with one hand before handing over a credit card. She hurried away, promising to return quickly with the receipt. Given that Max was basically ignoring her, she got points for being gracious.

Not once did Max look away from me during that brief exchange. "Okay what?" he asked.

"Okay, we'll let this play out."

I could tell my answer surprised him. His eyes widened slightly, his nostrils flaring, and he squeezed my hand lightly as his gaze darkened.

"Tell me the ground rules. I'm sure you have some," he said softly, his voice alone a seduction.

Before I could answer—and I didn't even know the answer—our waitress returned. Max signed the receipt and handed it back. If she had any thoughts about the fact he wasn't even acknowledging her, she didn't give it away. After a "Thank you," she left us.

Max stood from the table, curling his hand around mine more firmly. As I rose, I couldn't help but tease. "Are you going to let my hand go?"

He didn't reply, but then, he also didn't release my hand. Not that I minded.

As we began to walk out of the restaurant, he glanced down to me, a grin teasing the corners of his mouth. "No," he belatedly replied. "Beginning now, there won't be a moment when I'm not touching you. At least not for the next few hours."

The sensual promise contained in his words sent a rush

of heat rolling through me and an ache began to build at the apex of my thighs. The desire I'd been trying to tamp down was a brushfire rushing through my senses.

With his hand warm around mine, we walked through the reception area down to the bank of elevators. When we stepped into one, another couple followed us, and disappointment scored through me. It was a testament to the depth of my need for Max that I was frustrated I couldn't climb him like a tree right here in the elevator.

Let's be clear, I wasn't one for public sex, but Max hazed my mind and clouded my senses so thoroughly, I lost sight of everything but him. The space around us felt charged.

"Floor," he murmured softly.

"Oh, seven," I said, nudged out of my trance.

He jabbed the button and then leaned against the railing. At a glance, he appeared far more composed than I was. I felt as if I was tumbling and stumbling into a cauldron of desire. Meanwhile, he looked perfectly calm, cool, and collected. The only thing that gave anything away was the heat banked in his gaze when he glanced down to me.

The elevator ride felt like forever, although it couldn't have been more than a minute or two. The other couple's floor was above mine. As soon as the doors whispered shut behind us, Max moved swiftly, spinning me into his arms and against the wall.

"Thank fucking God you didn't tell me to leave tonight," he murmured, his words vibrating against my forehead. Then, his lips were ghosting across my skin, over my temple, and down along my cheek before they pressed against mine.

It felt almost as if he were breathing me in. With the feel of his hard, hot body pressed against mine and his elbows caging me against the wall, I was nearly out of my mind with need. When he started to draw back, a frustrated gasp slipped from my lips, and I snatched at his shirt, tugging him back to me.

He obliged. The moment his lips met mine again, his

tongue swept inside, and I moaned into his mouth. In a matter of seconds, our kiss was simply wild—our tongues tangling, stroke for stroke, hot, wet, and deep.

I lost track of everything but the feel of Max against me. His body was all muscle. His arousal rested at the juncture of my thighs, and I could feel every hard inch of him.

He muttered something into our kiss and then broke free. "Jesus, Harlow. I'm gonna fuck you right here against the wall. So unless you want that, you'd better tell me where your room is."

His words alone had my channel clenching. My panties had been soaked all through dinner, so that was nothing new. Through the haze of need, his words registered, and I managed to straighten and push away from the wall.

"Lead the way," he said, the rough edge of his voice sending butterflies spinning through my belly.

"This way," I murmured as I turned. A few steps along, I realized I'd gone the wrong direction and promptly did a U-turn, bumping into Max along the way. He didn't say a word, simply held tightly to my hand as I hurried down the hallway, my legs wobbly.

After pawing through my purse, I recalled my key card was in my pocket. Sliding it out, I scanned it over the sensor and then we were in my room. Max didn't wait. Spinning me against the door, our kiss picked up right where we'd left off. Only this time, there was nothing to hold us back.

By the time my brain came halfway online, my nipples were damp and he was swirling his tongue over a taut peak with my blouse and tank top in a rumple on the floor. My legs were curled around his hips as I rocked against his arousal.

"I need to get you naked," he murmured as he drew back from yet another punishing kiss.

Stepping back from the door, he held me high against him and I dragged my tongue along his neck, savoring the salty tang of his skin. Everything I had told myself about keeping my distance was lost in the maelstrom of the burning desire spinning around us, catching us in its flame.

I loved how easily he held me. He nudged the dimmer on the lights as he rounded the corner of the narrow hallway into my room. When we reached the bed, he eased me down. I stood immediately, kicking my boots free and shimmying out of my jeans. It was as if we were in a race to see who could get their clothes off the fastest. My boots ended up in two corners of the room, my jeans in a pile on the floor, and my underwear was tossed on the nightstand.

Then, he was stretching out on the bed beside me, and I was moaning at the feel of his hot skin against me. I was so frantic, I curled my legs around him, rolling on top to straddle him.

"I need you," I gasped.

Max gripped my hips, holding me still when I tried to rise up. "Oh, you have me. But I'm not rushing. You're meant to be savored."

Sweet hell. This man was going to slay me with words.

He rolled us over in one swift move, and my protest was lost in our kiss. Then his lips were trailing down my neck, his stubble scraping across my breasts as he swirled his tongue around my nipples, and his fingers were teasing between my thighs. I forgot that I meant to argue and got lost in a blur of sensation.

I hadn't known this about myself before my last night with Max, but I loved how he simply took control. Oh, he wasn't pushy, or domineering about it. In fact, his control was so complete, that was entirely unnecessary. As his teeth grazed over my nipple and I cried out, I felt his low chuckle against my skin.

He slid back up my body, his weight settling against me. I reflexively arched my hips into him. I was slick and wet, and his cock slid against my folds.

"Oh no, you can't make me rush," he murmured against

my lips. With another swipe of his tongue against mine, he drew back with a nip.

I nipped right back, eliciting another chuckle. "That's what I love about you," he murmured.

"What?" I asked, raw need lashing at me.

"You forget to be polite. Bite me all you want."

Before I could react, he was mapping his way down my body, his lips, teeth, and tongue teasing me, and his hands sliding down my thighs to press them apart. When his lips dusted across my belly, I cried out.

"Need something?" The sly tease in his voice only notched the need higher inside of me.

Rocking my hips restlessly, I murmured, "Yes."

When I glanced down, his blue eyes seared me. He trailed his fingertips across my slick folds, coasting over my clit, just enough to send a zing of pleasure through me and make me gasp.

"This maybe?" he asked as he finally, *finally*, sank a finger inside me.

I was so worked up, I almost came right then, but he gave me just enough to twist the need tighter and make my hips buck into him.

"Max," I murmured, close to anger.

Just like my night with him over a year ago, it was as if he knew when I had reached my limit. Another finger joined the first and he stroked, fucking me slowly with his fingers. His mouth joined in on the action and his tongue teased over my clit as he pumped in and out of me.

Merely spending time in the vicinity of Max was foreplay for me, so I was at the edge already, the wave curling tighter and tighter inside and crashing over me so hard I blacked out when the pleasure hit me.

As my mind flickered back online, I felt him draw away before he rose up over me. I had no idea where he got a condom, but he was rolling it on in no time before his weight settled over me.

It didn't matter he'd just sent me flying so hard I was nearly boneless—I wanted him inside of me. I started to curl my legs around him, but he shifted his weight, rolling us over so I was sitting astride. I felt exposed, bare to him as he looked up at me. Shimmying back, he rested against the headboard. With his dark gaze on mine, my heart thudded as he brushed my tangled hair away from my face.

"Ride me," he said.

There was no hesitation. I couldn't have said no to Max, not for anything when we were like this. As I rose up, he reached between us, dragging the thick head of his cock back and forth through my folds. I was so over-sensitized, I almost came again. But then, he surged inside as I sank down, the stretch of him filling me, drawing a rough cry from my throat.

His thumb traced over my lips, and I caught it in my teeth, opening my eyes when he murmured my name.

"I want you to know exactly who I am when you come," he said bluntly.

Dear God. *This* man. His hands slid down my sides to grip my hips. It started slow as I rocked into him and he surged up into me, every stroke a little deeper. I was tight, because it had been a damn year since I'd had sex.

I tumbled into the moment—the feel of his strong hands on my hips, my nipples brushing against his chest as I rose up and sank down—again and again and again. I was chasing after another release, this one building more slowly, more intensely.

I was chanting his name as pleasure began to unravel inside. His thumb circled over my clit, and I came with a quivering cry, distantly hearing his raw shout as he went taut and shuddered underneath me. His arms came around me and his hand tangled in my hair as I collapsed against him.

He was a touchstone in a spinning eddy of pleasure, the aftershocks echoing through my system.

Chapter Sixteen

MAX

I fell asleep tangled up in Harlow and woke up the same way. I didn't know what the hell I was doing. Not really. All I knew was I wasn't about to leave her side. It felt too fucking good to be with her. She was like a drug, with a straight line into my veins.

After we unraveled ourselves, I carried her to the shower. Once we were all washed up, we fell back into bed with her drifting off to sleep tucked against my shoulder, one of her calves hooked over mine. I'd lain awake for a while, contemplating how difficult it was to maintain my control when it came to Harlow.

I had never had to put too much effort into relationships. It had only become easier once I was a successful CEO with money and connections. Not that I cared all that much. Though I had money now, I'd been raised simply. My parents hadn't been flat-out poor, but they'd always just gotten by. My father was a mechanic and my mother, a teacher. I'd grown up in a medium-sized town in western Pennsylvania. The mountains there were beautiful, and life was simple.

Aside from excelling in sports, I'd been very bright. Had my father been in a different position when he was a boy, he could easily have become an engineer. My facility with those skills came from him, as did my quick work with numbers. As it was, he was a damn good mechanic and perfectly content with his life.

He and my mother had been high school sweethearts and raised me and my younger sister, Mariana, in a quiet, simple way. Coming from a caring family, I'd had a girlfriend in high school who I thought I loved. We parted on friendly terms when I went off to college, and then MIT.

That was where I met Cheryl. I'd wanted more for myself than what my parents had, yet I also wanted the stability they shared. Cheryl and I quickly settled into the kind of relationship you had in college and grad school—lots of sex and lots of studying.

I'd fancied myself in love with her, and I supposed I was. Then, I took her home with me one weekend. I didn't know what she expected, but I suppose she didn't expect the slightly rundown single-story ranch home, with a small yard and my dad's shop right there on the property.

It had been tense. I hadn't tried to create any other impression about my childhood, but in hindsight, I could see she might've expected something else. She was looking for money and had the brains to hope she could find it. To this day, I think she only stayed with me because of my high profile at MIT. I had the skills to land whatever position I wanted in engineering. When I didn't take a lucrative position as a software or systems engineer at a company paying high-dollar, she dumped me and told me she thought I was too simple for her.

It was nothing horrible, but it had certainly soured me. By that point, I was focused on work and building my own company, and money was tight. I'd poured all of my energy into that, and decided I didn't want to waste my time trying to find what my parents had.

Harlow shifted beside me, her silky skin sliding against mine. She didn't wake and settled against me on a soft exhale. I'd woken earlier with my arm curled around her and my palm cupping the generous curve of her bottom and been quite content to leave it there as my mind wandered.

Her subtle motion brought my mind back to the present. I wanted to convince myself that this was just sex. It was certainly a white hot, raw, primal attraction, and the sex was fucking amazing.

Yet, I hadn't forgotten the sense of relief after our night last year when I left. I now knew, even though I'd only had two nights with Harlow, I'd been kidding myself when I thought we could burn this to ashes. I had enough sense to know everything between us was made that much more powerful by the intensity and intimacy shimmering with it.

That begged the question as to why I didn't get up and leave this morning. Because relationships were business for me, but there was no way in hell I was walking away from Harlow. Not right now.

In fact, I was calculating what I would need to do to convince her not to write me off, not to box me out. I didn't know how, but I knew someone had hurt her, and I was determined to somehow assuage that pain. That made no fucking sense. Then again, nothing made sense with how I responded to Harlow.

I rolled my head to the side, glancing to the nightstand. The clock read seven a.m. It was still dark out, but then, we were in Alaska. December was days away. I idly wondered where Harlow had spent Thanksgiving and hoped she hadn't been alone.

Despite Ivy's worry about me over the holidays, I did have family, and they mattered to me. Quite a lot. Though Ivy had known me for a few years at this point, I doubted Owen chatted much about me.

Perhaps I'd had business meetings on Christmas Eve every so often, but it was only because of choice, not because I couldn't have gone home. Merely thinking about my family with Harlow warm against me had me wondering about her. I knew her mother died when she was young, so it had just been her and her father. Howard May was well-known for working at any and all times.

The part of my mind that had resolved not to bother with relationships put up a feeble argument.

What the hell are you thinking? You don't do this anymore.

Whatever part of my brain Harlow had activated had its own train of thought about that.

Hell yes, I do. Harlow doesn't want anything from me. Not money, not status. She could've had all that on her own just from her father, and she walked away from it.

A sense of unease ran through me, but I ignored it. I wasn't walking away from Harlow, even if what we had was just something to burn out. I would see it through until that happened. If there were more, I would see that through too.

I kicked my thoughts out of the weeds when Harlow shifted against me again, and I couldn't resist the urge to let my hands get busy. She was too soft, too fucking appealing. I slid my hand over the sweet curve of her bottom, trailing my fingers lightly over her silky skin.

Her nipple tightened against my chest. Two hands were quite convenient. Traveling up over her side, I teased her nipple with my thumb, sensing the moment she came awake. She murmured something against my skin and then rose up on her elbow. There was a hint of light filtering out from the entryway to the room where we'd left the light on last night. Her hair was a tangle around her face.

"What time is it?" she asked, her voice husky with sleep.

"Seven or so."

I brushed my thumb back and forth over her nipple, savoring the soft hitch in her breath. I wasn't sure what she was thinking, but I knew the moment she stopped. A little laugh escaped, and then she dipped her head and dusted kisses across my chest.

I meant to say something, but she moved swiftly. Shimmying down my body, she pushed the sheets out of the way. I let out a rough groan when she curled her palm around my cock.

Fuck me. This woman. I threaded my hand in her hair as she swirled her tongue around the head of my cock. She took me into the slick wet heat of her mouth, nearly making me come right then and there. I'd woken up hard because all she had to do was exist beside me and I wanted her.

She took me to the edge, pulling back to swirl her tongue around and dragging it along the underside before sucking me deep again. I was on the verge of exploding, but I wanted to be inside her.

"Harlow," I bit out.

She drove back, laughing softly in the shadowy room. "What?"

I moved swiftly, tugging her up and spinning us over. She giggled and my heart squeezed. "Hey, I was busy," she protested.

"I know. But I want to come inside of you."

She grinned and dipped her head, dragging her tongue along my neck and nipping with her teeth. Her legs were curling around my hips and her slick wet heat was tempting me. At the last second, I remembered I needed a condom.

"Fuck," I muttered, not letting her go as I rolled slightly on the bed, reaching for the jeans I'd kicked to the floor last night.

After a bit of fumbling, with Harlow teasing me, I managed to get a condom on. Then, I sank home inside of her.

I held still for a moment, savoring the feel of her channel clenching around me, and my heart thudded inside my chest, an unfamiliar intimacy curling like smoke around us. I didn't care to contemplate it. I just wanted to lose myself in Harlow.

She'd already had me so worked up, I was at the edge of

my restraint the moment I buried myself to the hilt. My release was twisting in the base of my spine inside of two strokes. Rushing wasn't my style. But then, there was no such thing as style when it came to Harlow and me. It was hot, quick, and dirty. Even when I savored every moment, it was a blur of madness.

I forced myself to draw back more slowly, gauging if she was as close to the edge as I was.

"Max, don't," she gasped.

"What?" I countered as I surged into her, clinging to a thin thread of restraint.

"Don't make me wait!" she cried out when I drove back again.

"Look at me."

I needed to see her fly apart in the shadows. Her eyes dragged open, her lids heavy. Somewhere along the way, I'd laced my fingers into hers with one hand. I held on to that anchor point. Reaching between us, I pressed against her slippery wet clit. Her hips bucked against me, and her walls clamped down around me, throbbing and pulsing as she cried out.

I finally let go, my release hitting me like a shock force. Shuddering, I fell against her, rolling us over so I didn't crush her. I was still buried inside her and didn't want to move. I shouldn't have needed her that much, not after last night. But then, I was beginning to wonder if my need for her would ever be slaked.

The sound of our breathing slowed as I sifted my fingers through her hair. Propping up on her elbow, she rested her chin on her hand. As she regarded me quietly, I wondered just what the hell she was thinking.

"How long are you in Anchorage?" she asked.

"It's looking like a month."

"You'll stay here through Christmas?"

"If I need to. I might leave to go see my family, but I'll

come back. There are usually a lot of logistical issues when we transition into management for a company."

In the realm of crazy, I considered asking her to come with me to see my family. Knowing she was estranged from her father didn't sit well with me, and I didn't like the idea that she might be alone on the holidays.

That was how fucking crazy I was about Harlow. I expected my rational brain to kick in here. I expected it so much, that I almost asked for its opinion. Yet, my rational voice, which had driven my decisions about relationships for years now and had compartmentalized them into a tidy file folder in my life, was strangely silent.

I was oddly okay with that.

Chapter Seventeen

MAX

After we untangled ourselves from each other and showered for a second time—where I had to beat back the urge to take her again—we dressed and went down to the lobby for breakfast together. With Harlow's dark brown hair damp from the shower and her eyes bright, she looked fresh-faced and young, far too pure for me. She shooed away the waitress with the menu, declaring she wanted the breakfast buffet.

Once we were seated, she glanced over from across the table, her cheeks pinkening slightly. "I like to eat," she murmured, gesturing to her plate.

For a moment, I was confused and then realized she was referencing her plate piled high. Seeing as I had more food on my plate than she did, obviously we were in agreement on that point. "I think I win this one," I countered.

I elected not to expound upon the fact that I didn't give a damn how much she ate, and sure as hell preferred a woman with curves for days. As we dug into our meals and sipped coffee, I glanced out the window. It was snowing and the pace was picking up rapidly.

"How long are you planning to be in Anchorage?" I asked, in between bites.

"Well, I was supposed to go back yesterday, but it got late. I'll probably head back in a little while."

I didn't like that answer. Glancing out the window again and back to her, I said, "I don't think today's a good day for a drive."

Harlow shrugged. "It's Alaska. There are more days than not where the weather's like this in the winter. I'll be fine."

Even though I sensed she didn't appreciate my observation, I was feeling stubborn and didn't care to consider why. "Harlow, do me a favor and don't drive in this."

She was midway to lifting her fork to her mouth and paused with the fork in midair. "Are you seriously asking me not to drive?"

She sounded quite shocked, and she had every reason to be. I wasn't usually the kind of man who would've shared my opinion on any woman's driving plans. But right now, I was disconcertingly worried about Harlow driving home in this weather.

I held her gaze and nodded before taking a gulp of my coffee and another bite of pancakes. She finished a bite and took a sip from her own mug, pausing to look out the windows. Snow was falling steadily, coating everything. There was no sky to be seen; nothing but slate gray as a backdrop against the white snow.

Her brown eyes cut back to me, narrowing. "Max, I'll be fine."

Her tone was steely and clear. I didn't even think about what I said next, it simply came out. "All right then, let me drive."

"What?!"

Max's steady gaze never wavered. "If you're going to insist on driving in this weather, I don't want you to go alone."

Taking a steadying breath, I mentally counted to ten and reached for my coffee to take a sip. "I can drive fine in this weather, Max. I've lived up here for a year now. This"—I paused, gesturing out the window at the snow—"happens all winter long."

"I wasn't implying you couldn't handle it. But the snow's coming down faster, and it's not exactly a short drive."

I took another sip of my coffee, honestly so startled by his suggestion and how ridiculous it was that I didn't even know how to respond. The annoying part was the idea of him coming home with me was quite appealing. I was ultimately irritated as hell that he didn't think I could handle the drive and also appreciative that he wanted to take care of me. Talk about a contradiction.

I rolled my eyes and took a bite of eggs. "That's ridiculous."

His eyes narrowed as he stared at me. "Okay then, let's compromise. You drive, but I come with you."

Now I just laughed. "Fine. How do you intend to get back? Plus, don't you need to be here?"

Max didn't even hesitate. "I can do whatever I want. We own the company. I've had a few days around the offices already, and I can do much of what I need to online."

I still thought the whole thing was ridiculous, but I shrugged. "Okay, fine. You ride with me. To a tiny town where I'm sure you'll be bored."

It was Max's turn to chuckle. "I won't be bored."

At the hot look in his eyes, my body tightened, heat blooming from my core. I didn't know what he was doing or why, but my body sure thought it was a good idea.

A few hours later, Max was climbing into my little truck. I recalled the last time I'd been in a vehicle with him—the afternoon of Ivy's wedding. The burning, yearning need for him had been almost instantaneous then, and hadn't faded in the least. I supposed I needed to count when he returned me to the hotel after the wedding, but I didn't remember that drive.

It was still snowing, and hard enough that if I'd been driving alone, I might've thought twice. I wasn't about to admit that to Max, though. I was actually a little relieved not to be by myself. It wasn't that far, but the drive to Willow Brook was along a largely empty stretch of highway once we got out of Anchorage.

I half-expected Max to comment on the conditions. The snow was thick, and falling at a steady clip from the sky. But he didn't.

Once we were in my small truck, he glanced over. "How long is the drive?"

"Forty-five minutes, give or take."

"Let's get this show on the road then."

After we'd eaten breakfast, he left the hotel to swing by the offices and take care of a few things. He returned to the hotel with a briefcase, a laptop in a traveling bag, a wheeled cart full of files, and an overnight bag. When I inquired about the files, he explained it was easier for him to go over things on paper than in the computer when it came to reviewing numbers.

Max's presence filled the space in my little truck. I didn't know what to make of the fact he was coming with me. The first part of the drive was quiet as I made my way out of Anchorage. Once I was on the highway heading west toward Willow Brook, Max spoke.

"Speaking of small towns, how do you like living in Willow Brook?"

Keeping my eyes on the road, I considered my answer. "I like it. I wasn't sure about it at first, to be honest. I don't know how much you know about my dad, but growing up, I mostly lived in hotels. He was always traveling and just took me with him."

I flicked my eyes sideways briefly to see Max looking at me, his gaze inscrutable.

"While I know your father, I've certainly never talked to him about his personal life, so I didn't know that."

"I suppose it's nice to just be in one place. Even though I sort of had a home base in North Carolina, where my mother was from, she died when I was six. I don't have anywhere that was really *home* growing up. Willow Brook is nice. It's pretty busy in the summer because of the tourists, and it's close enough to Anchorage that I can get my city fix if I need it."

"How did you meet Ivy?"

"I met her at a fundraising function in San Francisco that my father hosted. We hit it off, and we've been friends ever since."

I paused as I rounded a corner in the highway, slowing. Even my trusty little four-wheel-drive truck started to skid slightly. I wasn't about to tell Max he was right, but the roads were pretty slick. While the snow was beautiful as it fell, dusting the trees and the mountains with a fresh coat, it was the worst kind to drive in. I called it "snot" snow—that kind of snow that was just damp and heavy enough that it was like sliding in snot on the road, if that made any sense.

If Max had any thoughts about the road conditions, he didn't say anything. When I steadied the truck and glanced his way, his features were tense but he was quiet.

"It's not the best weather," I said, deciding there was no point in being passive and pretending like it was fine.

Max chuckled. "No, the weather's pretty bad, but you'll notice I didn't comment."

I burst out laughing. "Thank you for that. So tell me a little bit about your family."

I figured we might as well chat to keep me from white-knuckling the drive too much.

"My parents are still happily married, and I have a younger sister, Mariana. She travels a lot for her job as a journalist. My parents live in the same house where I grew up in western Pennsylvania. It's in the mountains, and it's beautiful. I might live in the city now, but the town I grew up in is small. Perhaps not as small as Willow Brook, but I know what small town life feels like. I'm not really a city boy myself."

"What do your parents do?"

"My dad runs a mechanic shop, right beside our house, and my mom is a teacher."

"And you're a crazy rich engineering investor. I guess I wouldn't have expected that."

Max chuckled again. "I suppose not. If my dad would have had more money when he was younger, or perhaps someone to push him in the different direction, he probably would've been a better engineer than me. I was a wild boy when I was young, but I was good in school and had a few teachers that pointed me in the right direction. I ended up at MIT on a scholarship. That's where I met Owen and a few other friends. My time there set my career on its path. I didn't intend to become as much of an investor as I am, but I'm good with numbers and making things work. I still enjoy design obviously, but it's not my mainstay."

I turned these new details about Max over in my mind, wondering how to make sense of him. I had categorized him in a way that perhaps wasn't fair.

We drove quietly for a bit, and I slowed as we approached the road that would lead us to Willow Brook. The weather was bad enough that I needed to stay focused. If Max thought anything of it, once again he stayed quiet. After we turned onto the side road and I slowed further, he spoke again. "Next time the weather is this bad, we're not driving in it."

What the ever-loving fuck?

A flash of anger rose inside. "Look," I began, with my hands tight on the steering wheel and never once looking away from the road, "we've made it just fine. We're almost there. Since when do you get a say in whether or not I drive in weather like this?"

"I'd tell *Owen* he was foolish to drive in this," Max retorted.

We rode in silence the rest of the way to Willow Brook, and I was quite relieved to turn onto Main Street. I took a deep breath, letting it out and willing the tension to ease from where it had bundled in my shoulders and neck.

"I need to make a few stops," I commented.

"Okay," was all he said in reply.

Chapter Nineteen

MAX

Although I sensed Harlow had formed a certain impression of me, it wasn't what she thought. While I had grown up in a small town, in a not-even-quite middle-class family, it was a bit of luck, some chance, and a lot of hard work that landed me at MIT, which had opened the doors that led to me being the man I was today. None of that meant I was an entitled and arrogant wealthy man.

My background aside, I couldn't quite say what prompted me to suggest I drive with her. I only knew I didn't want her to go alone and the sense of protectiveness driving that was like a tripwire in my brain. There were a few white-knuckle moments on the drive, but Harlow clearly knew how to handle her truck in the snow and ice. I was still relieved to be with her.

As she slowed once we reached Willow Brook, I glanced around. Although the snow was still falling steadily, the town was busy. The lights of the shops glowed through the gray afternoon. Holiday lights glittered through the snow where they were strong on the streetlights and shop fronts. It was a cute little town, with the Alaska Range as its backdrop in one direction and the ocean in the distance in the other.

Even through the snowfall, I could see the mountains looming, the jagged ridges and peaks rising above. I'd traveled up to Alaska a few times since Owen had relocated Off the Grid here. Though I hadn't seen all of the state, I was quite aware that most of the small towns here catered to tourists. Willow Brook was no exception, with cute storefronts and lots of retail shops mixed in with restaurants. Like Diamond Creek, where Owen and Ivy lived, I expected it was quieter in the winter, perhaps even more here because there was no ski lodge.

The roads here were clear, more so than the highway. I imagined the town's road crew stayed busy with their plow trucks all through the winter. Harlow drove straight through town, pulling into a building at the far end of the main street. The sign—Willow Brook Fire & Rescue—was barely visible with the snow coating it.

When I tossed my bags in the back, I'd noticed the back of her truck was full. As soon as she turned off the engine, she glanced to me. "You can wait, or you can come in."

"I'll come in."

Curiosity led the way when it came to Harlow. I knew, quite obviously, that this was the station where her crew was housed. I was curious to see a little bit more of her life. This should have given me pause, but then, I was breaking unspoken rules up, down, and sideways when it came to her.

Following her in, we stepped into a reception area, where a woman with a riot of brown curls and wide brown eyes smiled the moment she looked up.

"Harlow! You're back. Ward was just saying he wondered if you had the new engine block with you."

"Of course I do," Harlow replied as she strode across the room.

She was dressed in jeans and hiking boots with a fitted blue jersey shirt. Of course, what I had noticed this morning was the fact that her shirt unbuttoned just far enough that I was tempted to drag my tongue through the valley between her breasts.

I'd never paid much attention to what women wore. I was fairly certain Harlow could wear an actual brown sack, and I would find it sexy. She was *that* delectable. Her glossy dark hair was up in a ponytail, swinging between her shoulder blades.

She stopped at the counter surrounding the woman, leaning her elbows on it. "Is Ward busy?"

The woman nodded before her eyes flicked to me, blatant curiosity contained in her gaze. She didn't hold back. "Who are you? I'm Maisie."

With her round cheeks, her wide eyes, and a smattering of freckles, she was so adorable, it was impossible not to smile in return.

"I'm Max," I replied, reaching my hand across the counter. She looked surprised by that, but shook my hand rather vigorously.

"If you're a friend of Harlow's, you're a friend of mine. I didn't know you were bringing company," Maisie said, as she looked back to Harlow.

I felt Harlow's gaze on me and turned to her, winking. I wanted to tease her, and I didn't know why. Her espresso gaze darkened slightly and a flush crested on her cheeks.

Maisie opened her mouth to say something else when a door to the side of the reception desk opened. A tall, lanky man stepped through, his green gaze flicking from me to Harlow, and then to Maisie. Stepping behind the desk, he leaned down and kissed Maisie.

By the time he pulled back, her cheeks were flushed, and she rolled her eyes, pushing him away. "Good grief. I'm working."

The man looked to me. "Beck Steele," he said with a wink and a sly grin cast in Maisie's direction.

"Max Channing," I replied.

I sensed I was being assessed. I was just relieved it was clear this man was paired with Maisie. Ridiculous as it may have been, simply the sight of another man around Harlow sent a jolt of possessiveness through me. At some point, my sanity would kick in, but not just yet.

"Max is a friend of mine," Harlow added.

Oh, this *friend* bit was going to get to me. Not that I knew what my place was in Harlow's life, but "friend" didn't seem a satisfactory explanation. However, I knew a real quick way to piss her off would be to correct that publicly.

At this point, I should've been wondering what the hell I was thinking. But my common sense had fled the building, it seemed. My cock was driving this boat, and it said that Harlow was *far* more than a friend.

"You need some help getting that engine block in here?" Beck asked, looking to Harlow.

"I sure can't carry it myself," Harlow retorted with a grin.

"Pull around back," Beck replied.

"I can drive around back," I said, not even thinking whether that would be okay with Harlow.

She raised a brow slightly, but surprised me by simply handing over the keys. Within a minute or two, I had pulled her truck around to the back of the station, where I found her standing with Beck and several other men as the garage door rolled up.

Side note: I hadn't considered that her job as a hotshot firefighter essentially meant she was surrounded by rugged, strong men all day. I wasn't sure I liked that idea so much.

Dude, pump the brakes. Since when were you possessive?

Since Harlow was mine. My mental reply was swift.

Truth be told, I knew part of the driving force for me with Harlow was lust, but there was another deeper force layered under that, one I wasn't quite ready to examine.

Figuring it was the sensible thing to do, and knowing my dad would've kicked my ass at his garage if I didn't, I backed the truck into the garage, rolling the window down to call out and ask how far they wanted me to go. I recognized Beck's voice when he replied, and followed his hand signals in the rear view mirror, stopping when he indicated.

Harlow was already opening the back of the truck and pointing to what I gathered was an engine block. It was no wonder she had good traction on the slick roads with the weight of it in the back. I didn't grow up around a mechanic to be oblivious to the weight of an engine block.

Beck had stepped in, along with another man who had black hair and silvery gray eyes. His gaze cut to me. "Ward," he said, simply nudging his chin up.

"Max. You guys need some help?"

"Sure thing, there's only three of us, and this thing weighs a fucking ton," Beck said with a wry smile.

Another man approaching caught my eyes. "I'm Jesse, by the way."

"Max," I repeated.

"I can help," Harlow said, stepping to the back of the truck's tailgate.

Ward looked from her to me. "Don't take this the wrong way, Harlow. I know you can handle yourself at a fire as well as any of us, but this is brute strength. Max is stronger."

Harlow rolled her eyes, but she didn't argue and stepped back. With Beck and Jesse lifting on one side, and Ward and I on the other, we carefully moved the engine block out of her truck onto a heavy-duty steel table right beside it.

"Thanks, man," Ward replied, as we all collectively stepped back. Ward looked to Harlow. "And thanks for picking this up. We need it for one of the old brush trucks. Change of plans, by the way. You're off for the rest of the week."

"Oh, why?" Harlow asked quickly.

"We changed up the rotation because I need time off for the holidays, so Beck's crew is covering. Enjoy it. Looks like you've got company anyway."

I didn't know why, but it was clear this bothered Harlow. She didn't say anything though and just shrugged. "Okay."

"What brings you here?" Jesse asked conversationally.

"He's a friend of Harlow's," Beck explained.

I might've known Beck for a whopping total of five minutes at best, but even I could sense the sly tone in his voice and see the gleam in his eyes. No doubt he was a perceptive man and had picked up on the electricity zinging between Harlow and me.

"You should join us tonight," Jesse added.

"For what?" Harlow asked, her eyes bouncing to him.

"Dinner at Wildlands. It's Em's birthday tomorrow, so she'd love for you to be there," he explained.

Whether Harlow would've wanted me to go or not, I sensed she felt cornered. She nodded though, which surprised me a bit.

"Of course we'll be there for Em's birthday. What time?"

"Six o'clock."

Harlow nodded and turned to climb in her truck, pausing when she reached in her pocket. Turning to me, she held out her hand, and I tossed the keys over.

"We'll see you guys later," she called over her shoulder.

"Nice to meet everyone. Sounds like I'll be seeing you later," I said, casting my gaze around.

Beck winked, Ward nodded, and Jesse grinned. I almost laughed. Even though my territorial urge was pulsing right under my skin, I didn't sense any of these guys had a thing for Harlow. I didn't care to contemplate how fucking insane it was that I was even thinking like that. Only one word came to mind when I thought of Harlow.

Mine.

Chapter Twenty

HARLOW

When I rolled my truck to a stop in front of the house, I experienced a flash of uncertainty. I kicked it away, reminding myself that while Max might have money now, I'd since learned he hadn't been raised with it. In fact, his childhood had certainly been more simple than mine. I didn't need to wonder what he might think about my small home here in Willow Brook.

Snow was piled high on the steps and porch, and I glanced over to see Max looking curiously around the yard. The snow had slowed its pace enough that some of the yard was visible. The cabin I'd rented from Susannah was a small A-frame. It was fairly new and had purple trim and a bright green roof, which stood out in the snowy landscape. It sat in a small clearing, with spruce trees, cottonwood, and birch scattered about the clearing and then thickening into the wilderness behind the house.

From the front of the home, the mountains were visible in the distance, their peaks looming above the tree line. Max's gaze circled back to me. "I'll help shovel," he said.

I didn't know what I expected him to say, but it wasn't that. A surprised laugh escaped. "No need."

He opened his door, climbing out quickly. I followed and caught his reply. "I'm not going to just stand around while you do it," he called over his shoulder.

Fetching our bags out of the back of the truck, Max walked with me to the house. The sound of our footsteps was muted through the snow as we walked onto the porch. Since I'd left yesterday, a good foot of snow had fallen. Stepping through the side door into the kitchen, I knocked the snow off my boots and tossed my bag on the floor while Max did the same. I snagged a pair of gloves out of a little basket on a table by the door, intending to take care of clearing the steps right away.

Just when I thought Max wouldn't be able to help me shovel because I couldn't imagine he had gloves, he reached into his bag and took a pair out, snagging a hat in the process.

When he caught me looking his way, he winked. "You know, this isn't my first time in Alaska. Plus, I plan to do some skiing while I'm here."

Tugging his gloves on, he followed me back outside. I handed him a shovel, and he got right to work. Inside of a few minutes, he'd cleared the snow from the deck and steps, while I shoveled a path to the parking area. I had a plow guy who would likely come by sometime this evening to take care of the driveway. Fortunately, my four-wheel drive truck could make it through the snow that had fallen so far.

Once we returned inside, I quickly showed him around. "I rent this place," I offered by way of explanation as I circled my arm around the downstairs. When I started to walk up the stairs, Max snagged our bags without me even asking.

I didn't know what to think of any of this. I felt as if I was suspended in time. Of all the men I would've expected to want to spend time in Willow Brook with me, Max Channing might've been dead last on that list.

Not that there was anyone on that list, to be honest. I had no idea what to make of his presence here. It felt as if everything with us was like a ball rolling down a hill. I didn't know where it was going to bounce, or what was going to happen. The momentum of it just kept pushing me forward.

I showed him the guest room and bathroom first before moving to my bedroom. Stepping through the door, I glanced around. I hadn't decorated much. I really hadn't had anything I could call my own bedroom when I was growing up. I'd left up a few photographs that Susannah had left from around the area, and hung a watercolor from my mother. She had loved to paint.

A queen-size bed piled high with pillows, with a matching dresser of light ash wood and two nightstands, were the extent of the furnishings in the bedroom. Max set our bags down in front of the dresser. I felt a wash of uncertainty. He was so confident, so certain, and I didn't even know what to think. With my anxiety driving me, I spun around and hurried back down the stairs.

"Do you want something to drink before we go back into town?" I called over my shoulder.

Max didn't reply until we were both back in the kitchen as I swung open the door to the refrigerator. "It looks like we're going to have to turn back around soon," he commented.

"You gonna tell me we shouldn't drive in this weather?" I teased.

His mouth curled into a grin, sending butterflies spinning in my belly. With a shrug, he shook his head. "No. It's not far. Who is Em, by the way?"

"Oh, that's Emily. She's Charlie's daughter, and Charlie happens to be Jesse's fiancée. Em works at the fire station, so we all know her. She's fifteen going on thirty. She's a sweet kid and pretty funny too. I hope you don't mind that I'd like to go."

"Of course I don't mind. It's obvious she's important to you. Plus, it's not like you expected my company."

His gaze was penetrating as he regarded me. I felt suddenly nervous again. I didn't really know how to do this. Not to mention that I didn't know what *this* was.

"What are we doing, Max?" I blurted out.

The moment my question escaped, I wanted to snatch it back. Sometimes thought bubbles jumped out of my head without my express permission. As his eyes coasted over my face, I didn't how to read his expression.

"I'm here because I didn't like the idea of you driving alone in today's weather. But I don't think that's what you're asking. Am I right?"

My heartbeat was thumping erratically. I hadn't been involved in anything remotely resembling a relationship in too long. I didn't know what to call this.

Max was way out of my league. I didn't know what to do with how much I wanted him. I had guarded myself so thoroughly, I was unprepared for anything other than the lowest possible expectations. In this case, that would have been the one night-stand Max and I enjoyed a year ago. This—him, here, in my home—was far too confusing for me to interpret. I marshaled my courage and took a deep breath, squaring my shoulders.

"What did you mean when you said you wanted to see where this went?"

He was quiet, his eyes never once shifting away from mine. Max was not a man who had trouble with eye contact. It was rather disconcerting to have his intense gaze solely focused on me.

He finally laughed softly, almost as if to himself. "I'm not entirely sure. I just know..." He paused as he pushed his elbow off the counter where he'd been leaning on the island and rounded it. I was standing in front of the refrigerator with my hand on the door handle, as if it could hold me up. I certainly needed something to help stay strong, and I suppose the refrigerator was as good as any other metaphorical option at this point.

Max stopped right in front of me. Without even an ounce of hesitation, his hands rested on my waist. In a hot second, he spun me around and slid my hips onto the island behind us. "I've noticed you worry a lot," he said, the rough velvet of his voice brushing over my skin and sending a prickle down my spine. Stepping between my knees, he slid his hands down over my hips, giving one of them a gentle squeeze.

"Maybe," I replied, uncertain where he meant to go with this.

"When I said maybe we should let this play out, I meant that we're a fire all on our own. That doesn't come along very often. I pride myself on not being foolish and not being stupid. I think it would be both if we ignored it," he said flatly.

Mere inches apart, he tugged me a little closer to the edge of the counter. I felt the hard, hot length of him pressing against my core. In a flash, I was needy and greedy all over again. It shouldn't be this ridiculous. I'd had more sex in the last twenty-four hours than in the last two years, with the exception of my one other night with Max. I idly wondered if perhaps I had forgotten how great sex could be.

Ha. Now that's stupid. Max is the best sex you ever had. No questions, no doubt, no argument.

It was rare I knew something with that much certainty, but I didn't even bother to engage in an internal debate over it. I *knew* what I had with Max was as rare as catching lightning in a bottle.

"Tell me you don't want me," Max said, his icy gaze darkening as he slid a hand up under my shirt and cupped one of my breasts.

A little sigh escaped from my lips when he teased my

nipple, his thumb brushing over the aching peak through the thin silk of my bra. My panties were drenched, and I wanted him all over again. I knew it wouldn't be enough. I didn't know if it would ever be enough.

While I might've wanted to tell myself I shouldn't give in, the current of desire running between us was so strong I couldn't swim against the tide. So I snatched what little control I had, deciding to harness the power rather than resist it.

Shimmying a little closer, I curled my legs around his hips, sliding my hand through the hair at his nape, and tugged him down for a kiss. My control was short-lived because once he swept his tongue into my mouth, I was lost. Kisses with Max were like tumbling into madness. Need slid through my veins and fire shimmered under the surface of my skin. Our tongues tangled, and he slipped his hand around my waist, cupping my ass and rocking his hips into me.

After a deep stroke of his tongue against mine, he drew back, catching my lower lip in his teeth. When I stepped back, I felt bereft for a moment. I'd been so caught up in our kiss, I was dizzy from it. It was like trying to stand after spinning in a circle too many times. I couldn't catch my balance.

Then, he was lifting me again and setting my feet on the floor. "Lose the jeans," he ordered softly.

Chapter Twenty-One

HARLOW

When we were in the heat of it and Max told me to do something, I simply did it. Flicking the buttons free, I kicked my boots off as I shimmied my jeans down and tossed them aside. Before I had a chance to even look at him, he was lifting me again and dragging his fingers over the wet silk between my thighs as he settled my hips back on the counter.

"We don't have much time," he murmured against my lips, his voice thrillingly low. I was a mess of need, panting and gasping, with my pulse running wild. "So I'm going to make you come, and you're gonna wish I had my cock buried inside of you. Then, you'll think about it for a few hours. By the time we come home later, maybe, just maybe, you'll want me as much as I want you."

Oh. My. God. When Max talked dirty, I gushed. My body was pretty much on high idle anytime I was near him. Little sparks of electricity were zipping and zapping through me. When he said things like that, I was lost in the riptide of desire, pulled swiftly under, and tossed asunder.

"Not fair," I murmured against his lips as he drew back from another punishing kiss.

He teased over the wet silk between my thighs, circling my clit. "You're fucking soaked. I've been hard for hours, and I'll be hard for a few more."

Then, he shoved the silk out of the way and buried two fingers knuckle deep inside me, and I cried out, my hips arching into him. He stepped closer, circling his thumb over my clit, which was hot, slick, and swollen from my juices. He leaned his forehead against mine.

"Tell me you don't want this," he repeated, echoing his earlier statement.

"Pretty sure I answered," I muttered, my pussy throbbing around his fingers as he drew them out slightly and then buried them inside of me again.

"Not in words," he murmured, his fingers drawing out and sinking inside yet again.

I knew he was trying to push me to simply state the truth. I wrestled against it, but it was pointless. When he drew his fingers all the way out and held still, teasing lightly over my folds, I dragged my eyes open.

"You're teasing me."

Pleasure was firing inside me, sensation scattering in sparks through my body. With the heat of him caged between my knees, I was just useless. I'd never imagined a man could make me come from a look, but it might be possible with Max. His gaze nearly burned me. My lower belly clenched and my pussy throbbed. My thighs were damp from my juices.

"I'm just trying to get you to admit how much you want me. Here." He caught one of my hands in his, putting it over his cock. It was hard and hot, pressing against his zipper. I felt it pulse against my palm and wanted him inside of me so desperately, I nearly cried out.

"I'm ready to explode, and I'm gonna fucking wait. I'm

not sure why. I just think it'll be that much better tonight, a few hours later. I want you more than I've ever wanted anyone, Harlow."

His words were raw and honest, and I sensed Max wasn't usually this blunt, not about things like this. I couldn't look away, a rushing sensation pouring through me. "I can't tell you I don't want you. Because I'd be lying," I finally said.

There was more to say, so much more, but I wasn't ready. Thank fucking God he buried his fingers inside me again, and began to fuck me hard and fast with them, drawing them in and out with his thumb teasing over my swollen clit.

My orgasm crashed through me so hard, my mind went blank. His name came on a rough shout. His lips collided with mine, capturing my ragged cries in our kiss.

He slowly drew away as my body shuddered, pleasure wracking me. I wanted more, just as he had predicted.

We stared at each other, sweet sensation eddying in my core. His gaze was dark. Reaching between us, I cupped my palm over his cock, gripping lightly through the denim. His breath came out in a hiss through his teeth.

"Not now."

Restless, I arched toward him, sliding my other hand around his nape and bringing him close. "You know you want me. Why deny it?"

He chuckled softly. "Because we're going to be late."

He stepped back swiftly, leaning over and snagging my jeans in his hand. I wanted to argue, but I also knew he was right. Shimmying my hips off the counter, I landed lightly on the floor. Taking my jeans from him, I slipped them on quickly. In another moment, I had my boots back on and glanced over at him. "Do you want to drive, or do you want me to?"

"I'll drive. You've driven enough for today."

I tossed him the keys, and he followed me toward the door. After we shrugged our jackets on, we stepped outside to snow still floating down from the sky. In a few minutes, we'd brushed the flakes off the truck and were driving back into Willow Brook. I directed him where to go, and he rolled to a stop in the parking lot behind Wildlands. A popular fishing and hunting lodge, Wildlands was situated on Swan Lake. Beyond hosting tourists in luxurious hotel rooms, the lodge had space for conferences and also had a popular local restaurant and bar.

As we stepped out of the truck, Max turned to look toward the lake behind the lodge. Swan Lake was the centerpiece of Willow Brook. The town's namesake was a brook that ran down from the mountains and fed into the massive lake. By virtue of my job as a hotshot firefighter, I'd gotten to know the geography of Alaska, perhaps more quickly than I would have otherwise.

Central Alaska was dotted with lakes, small and large. Swan Lake was one of the larger lakes in the area, with lodges surrounding it on three sides and the wilderness on the far side away from town. In the summer, the lake was busy with tourists, float planes were landing throughout the day, and people meandered on the walkways along the lake's shoreline.

This evening, with the snow falling through the darkness, the lake was barely visible, with the lights from the lodges circling it, glittering through the snow and mapping its shape in night. Max caught my hand in his as we stepped out of the truck, gesturing toward the lake. "I presume that looks a little different in the summer. I imagine the view is beautiful."

"Of course, but then, just about every view is beautiful in Alaska. It's much busier in the summer."

Turning away, he nodded as we began walking toward Wildlands Lodge. "I've visited Ivy and Owen in Diamond Creek in the summer. It's nuts. They stay busy year-round with the ski lodge now, but even then, winter doesn't hold a candle to summer as far as tourists."

Our conversation was cut off as we reached the back entrance. A cluster of people was leaving, and Max held the door for them, gesturing for me to walk in ahead of him. Once we were in the hallway that led into the restaurant and bar, he curled his hand around mine again. I wasn't quite sure what to think of him being this public with his affection. Not that holding someone's hand was major, but I'd been resolutely single for two years, so it felt kind of major for me. Seeing as the status of *us* was rather undefined, I didn't know how to interpret anything. With my body still humming from the orgasm he'd given me just before we left, I wasn't quite ready to try to set boundaries.

When we reached the back of the bar, Max paused and looked to me.

"This way," I said, leading the way as we threaded through the tables over to the restaurant area.

The lodge was in a massive timber frame style building with hardwood floors, exposed beams, and windows running along the side of the restaurant that faced the lake. Booths ran along the walls, with the bar and a section of pool tables on one side, and the restaurant with large round tables on the other. Holiday decorations added a festive touch, with bright red bows hung here and there, and holiday lights circling the bar and running along the exposed beams.

Em squealed when she saw me, standing from the table and hurrying over to fling her arms around me. Only then did Max let go of my hand as I returned her hug. Stepping back, I squeezed her shoulders with a grin. "Happy birthday. How old are you again?" I teased.

"Sixteen!"

Emily started coming to the station for community service after getting in a spot of trouble at high school. She'd been skipping classes and smoking cigarettes. She'd done her community service at the station, and then Rex Masters, the Chief of Police, offered her a job at the station, which was essentially doing anything that needed to be done. She helped out in the police station and the fire station, and her current career goal was to be a hotshot firefighter.

Her wide gray eyes bounced from me to Max, her curiosity completely obvious.

"Hi, I'm Em," she said, holding her hand out. She kept her almost-black hair short, and it was tipped with violet all over. She looked like a pixie with her fair skin, gray eyes, and slender build.

I'd rarely seen Max interact with a child, unless I counted the few passing encounters where I'd seen him around other people's children. Teenagers were another breed altogether.

He didn't miss a beat and flashed a grin, reaching out to shake Em's hand firmly. "I'm Max, and apparently I'm here to celebrate your birthday. I hope it's okay that I'm crashing the party."

Em was delighted with that, her smile widening and her eyes sparkling. "Of course it's okay!"

I braced myself for the next natural question, but Max reached for my hand, his warm strength curling around it.

"Oh, so you're dating," Em said, her curious gaze bouncing to me.

I opened my mouth to protest, but Max cut me off. "We are. I've known Harlow for a while. We met through a friend."

My cheeks felt hot, and I rolled my eyes. I wasn't too interested in letting Em ask a ton of questions. She was a curious teen and didn't hold back.

"Em, tell us where to sit," I said, scanning my gaze around the table.

Jessie and Charlie were bantering about something to do with the presents. Beck and Maisie were seated beside them, and Maisie was teasing Amelia about something. Lucy Phillips and her husband Levi were also there. She was on her phone, while he nibbled on some French fries. Em pointed us over to a pair of chairs between Lucy and Levi and Maisie and Beck.

As we rounded the table, it occurred to me that every-body here was paired up. I supposed even Max and I were, given what appeared to be his public claim.

Leaning back in my chair, I slid my hand along Harlow's shoulder to tease the soft skin at the back of her neck. Goose bumps rose under my fingers, and I loved knowing my touch affected her. Tonight was turning out to be an exercise in restraint. I didn't know what the hell I'd been thinking when I had held back earlier tonight. As it was, my cock was rock-hard right now and had been for most of the evening.

Thank fuck the table obscured my state. Harlow wasn't doing a thing to tease me, yet she had me strung tight with need by doing nothing more than sitting beside me.

I hadn't known what to expect, coming to meet with her friends here. But they were an easy bunch to be around, and all clearly loyal to each other. It made my heart clench a little to see Harlow hold herself back. She seemed almost surprised to be so fully accepted into the group. I was piecing together more of her childhood, though, so it was no wonder. Her father hadn't given her any sense of place or belonging. Knowing Howard as I did, business was about all he cared about. Dragging his little girl, who had lost her mother, all over the place, staying in hotels, seemed cold and thoughtless.

Harlow laughed at something Maisie said, reaching out to tuck a loose lock of her glossy brown hair behind her ear. Levi, who had introduced himself earlier, commented, "So, you and Harlow?"

By this point, I'd been grilled up and down, back and forth, and sideways. I knew her friends were screening to make sure I wasn't an asshole. I didn't know quite what to think of that. Yet, I was the one who'd pushed to make it public we were together. I didn't care to let it be seen any other way. I glanced at Levi, catching his dark blue gaze.

"Yes," was all I offered.

"She's a damn good firefighter," he replied, shifting gears.

"I would imagine."

If Levi hadn't been so obviously enamored with his pregnant wife, I might've felt territorial. As it was, I felt like I had to prove myself time and time again to these men. They now knew I had been raised by a mechanic and could navigate my way around most vehicles. There was the thinnest hint that perhaps being a CEO of a company wasn't tough enough, but they let it slide. Levi had actually hired Owen to design his house, which turned out to be a mark in my favor, especially when I got to tell him that a few of the designs he used came from work Owen and I had done together a few years back.

Levi nodded, and Lucy poked him in his side with her elbow. Though he was tall, lanky, and strong, and she was petite and pregnant, it was quite clear she was the one in charge. Levi didn't seem to care one whit about that.

"Good grief, you guys have grilled him enough tonight. He's here with Harlow, and that's fine," Lucy said. She caught my eyes, rolling her own. "Levi's a bit ridiculous. You should've seen him when his sister fell in love. Just happened recently, and he still hasn't quite gotten over it. There are only two female firefighters among the crews here, so they're a little protective." Lucy shrugged and laughed. "I guess Harlow is the last one for them to be bossy about. Unless you count Em, but she's too young."

Em called from across the table, the lights catching on the purple in her hair. "I'm not too young. I have a boyfriend now."

Jesse looked at her, but he didn't say a word. I could tell from the expression on his face he had some thoughts about that, but Charlie commented on something, quickly moving the subject along. Em got back to opening the last of her presents.

Harlow said something, and I glanced at her. "Yeah? I missed that."

She glanced to her watch and then outside the windows adjacent to our table. "I was just thinking we should get going before it gets too late. It's still snowing," she explained, pointing out the obvious.

The lights from the lodge illuminated the snow falling, glittering brightly in the darkness. "I thought snow didn't slow anything down?" I teased.

She laughed softly. "It doesn't usually change my plans, but it doesn't mean I want to be out too late in the dark on icy roads."

"Should we go now?"

She nodded, and it was then I realized her cheeks were flushed. I hoped like hell she was as hot and bothered as I was hard tonight. Because I knew what I would be doing once we got back to her place.

"Let's go then," I said, sliding my chair back.

We said our goodbyes, and I reached over for her hand as we turned to walk out. She didn't swat me away, although I sensed she was a little startled by the gesture. *I should've been, but I wasn't.* I was quite purposefully staking a claim, more for her benefit than anything.

Harlow assented to me driving again, and we drove home through the dark snowy night. The roads were definitely *not* good; slick, with ice forming as the temperature dropped. I was relieved I had experience driving through the winding mountain roads of Pennsylvania when I was younger. By no means was Pennsylvania like Alaska in the winter, but the mountains there got plenty of snow and the roads were narrow.

By the time we reached her house, it looked as if another six inches had fallen since we'd left earlier. We probably could've shoveled her deck again, but she told me it could wait until morning when I offered.

With nothing else in sight, it felt as if we were alone in the world as we walked into her cabin. I could see a few lights from other homes flickering through the trees, but nothing was close by. There was something about the snow and the wildness of this place that created a sense of isolation.

Once we were inside, we both kicked off our boots and hung our jackets by the door. Harlow hurried over to a small woodstove, quickly making a fire. Meanwhile, I checked the heat and flicked on a few lights.

She walked toward me, light and shadows playing over her skin. With a mind of their own, my eyes immediately dipped down to the shadowed valley between her breasts. I wasn't going to be satisfied with anything quick now. I needed to see every inch of her. I needed to savor her.

I didn't wait. The moment she was close enough, I reached out and caught her hand, reeling her into me. She came against me with a soft exhalation, her cheeks flushing.

"So tell me, Harlow, do you want more?"

The moment I spoke, the air around us charged to life, weighted with the electricity of desire shimmering around us. Her tongue darted out to swipe across her bottom lip. Her cheeks were stained pink, her eyes dark.

"I want more."

Damn. *This* woman. She surprised me time and again. I

expected her to be shy, to try to gloss over it. She poured gasoline on the fire of my need for her when she didn't.

"I need to see all of you," I said flatly. My tone came out harsher than I intended, but then Harlow had that effect on me. She brought everything right to the surface—my feelings for her were so primal, so elemental.

Tugging her hand loose from mine, she stepped back. Within a minute, she was stripping bare, tossing her clothes here and there on the floor around her.

Then, she stood before me, completely naked. I let my greedy gaze coast over her. Her skin was flushed, her full breasts round and plump. Her nipples were taut, practically begging for me to suck them. I loved the soft curve of her belly and the way her hips flared out.

She was sturdy and strong, the flex of her muscles evident as she stepped toward me, her eyes narrowing. "This doesn't seem quite fair, Max. You have too many clothes on. Lose them."

Funny, but when she told me what to do, I just did it. I usually liked to direct the action, yet Harlow always kept me barely at the edge of my control. With an assist from her, my clothes ended up scattered about the room with hers, and then she was pushing me, startling me when she nudged me back onto the couch.

Resting a hand on her hip, her rich brown gaze skimmed over me. My cock ached. In a flash, she knelt before me, sliding a palm up my thigh to cup my cock in her fist. She dipped her head, swirling her tongue around the thick head, swiping up the drop of pre-cum rolling out.

My head fell back against the couch, on the heels of a ragged groan, just as her hot, wet mouth took me inside. I needed to see. With effort, I lifted my head, threading a hand into her hair as she proceeded to drive me to the brink of madness. Teasing me with her lips and her tongue, and taking me into her mouth again and again, the light suction nearly pushed me over the edge.

This woman. She was like a straight line to everything I'd ever wanted. So reserved and so guarded that when she let go, it was like getting caught in a fire. I meant to say something, to pull her up and bury myself deep inside of her, but I was too lost in the feel of her mouth sucking me in as she cupped me lightly in her wet grip.

I heard myself murmuring her name, my hand tangling in her hair as I held on. Heat twisted at the base of my spine before she sucked me into her mouth once more, and my release poured into her. When she drew back slowly with a last swipe of her tongue around the head of my cock, I looked down to see her lips plump and swollen. Even though I had just come in her mouth, it had barely taken the edge off my need.

I loosened my hand in her hair, trailing my fingertips down along her jaw. As I traced her lips, she caught my fingertip in her teeth lightly, a sly grin stretching across her face.

"That's what you get for teasing me tonight."

"Oh, that's what I get? I'll tease you every day, sweetheart. Come here," I murmured, shifting slightly and lifting her toward me.

I think she presumed I wanted her to straddle me. I did, if only for the logistics of rolling over. I wanted to savor her, to drive her to the edge of madness, to make her beg.

As soon as her knees flanked my thighs, I shifted, rolling us quickly and stretching out over her. Her gasp of surprise was welcome.

"*This* is what you get for teasing me."

I caught her lips in a kiss, burying my tongue in her mouth, needing to claim her. Tearing my lips free, I dragged my tongue down along the soft skin of her neck. I needed to taste her tight little nipples. Shifting my weight, I mapped my way down her body. Teasing my thumb across one nipple, I swirled my tongue around the other, nipping it lightly and sucking it in, savoring when she arched into me.

Her hand gripped my hair as I proceeded to do the same to the other side. Leaning back, I looked down at her. She was propped partly against the cushions, her dark hair a wild tangle. The fire from the woodstove in the corner flickered over her skin, casting her in both light and shadow.

With her eyes dark, her lips swollen, and her skin flushed, she was so fucking gorgeous, I almost came again just looking at her. I knew she was wet. I could feel the slick heat of her rubbing against my cock where my hips rested in the cradle of hers.

"Max," she muttered. "Please..."

"Oh no, you'll have to wait."

Leaning forward, I swirled my tongue around a nipple again and began making my way down over her soft belly. I had one hand gripped on her hip and could feel her skin pebbling under my touch. Shifting my shoulders down between her knees, I leaned back to look. Her pussy was wet, pink, and glistening. I trailed a finger through her folds, savoring as her hips flexed into me automatically.

"You're so fucking wet. Tell me, have you been wet all night? Because I've been hard just about all day."

I wasn't prone to telling women how much they got to me. But then, no woman other than Harlow had ever kept me hard all day. It didn't even matter that I'd just exploded in her mouth; I was already hard again, hanging on to a thin, frayed thread of control.

Sinking a finger inside her, I savored the feel of her slick channel clenching around me. Adding another, I leaned forward because I *had* to taste her. Fucking her slowly with my fingers, I circled my tongue over her clit, through her folds, and proceeded to drive her as mad as she had just driven me.

Her release came quickly, her hands tugging roughly on my hair as her hips bucked into me. When I felt her channel start to throb and pulse around my fingers, I sucked her clit into my mouth, feeling her shudder as she cried out my name.

I'd never given a damn if a woman called my name. When it came to Harlow, I fucking loved it. I didn't want this to end. I wanted her to roll from one climax into the next. Drawing back swiftly, I rose above her, positioning my cock at her entrance and sinking inside in one swift surge.

Chapter Twenty-Three

HARLOW

Still trembling from my last climax with pleasure spinning through me, I was boneless, simply melted, from Max's attentions. Then, he sheathed himself inside me, every long, thick inch of him filling me to the hilt.

I barely caught my breath before he began to draw back and sink inside again. The weight of him above me felt so good—hard, strong, and encompassing. With his elbows caging my shoulders, he brushed my tangled, damp hair away from my face.

"Harlow, look at me," he murmured, his sensual command one I couldn't deny.

Dragging my eyes open, I collided with his gaze. In the flickering light from the fire, his blue eyes were dark, the look contained there so intense, it took my breath away. He stroked into me again as I curled my legs around his hips. He fucked me so thoroughly and so deeply, I was lost in a tornado of sensation.

My next climax began to build from the echoes of the last, the pleasure spinning inside, tighter and hotter with every roll of his hips into mine. Again and again, he filled me, the stretch exquisite. The entire time, our gazes were locked together, the sense of intimacy so intense I could hardly bear it.

The pressure spun loose, sending pleasure scattering through me like hot sparks. Max followed me over the edge, my name a rough shout. He fell against me, instantly rolling to his side, so that his weight wasn't heavy on me. I wanted to tell him that I didn't care, that I loved the feel of him against me, but I couldn't even form words.

We lay still, our skin damp and our breath ragged in the quiet room. After a beat, I felt Max tense slightly. Opening my eyes, I started to ask what was wrong, but he answered before I got a word out.

"I forgot a condom," he said flatly, his gaze somber and concerned.

"It's okay, I have an IUD," I explained hastily.

It wasn't that I needed one. I didn't exactly have an active sex life. But after my last unexpected pregnancy after missing a single pill while I was out in the field, I'd decided I needed something that wouldn't be affected by my unpredictable schedule.

His eyes searched my face, and I could feel his shoulders rise and fall with a deep breath. Brushing my hair away from my face, his mouth twisted ruefully. "Well, that's good, but I don't usually forget things like that. If you're concerned, I'm clean. This is the first time I've had sex without a condom since I was a teenager. At least then, I had the excuse of being stupid," he said with a low chuckle.

"I'm clean too. Not that you're asking, but except for you, I haven't had sex in two years. I suppose this means we don't need to worry about condoms anymore."

I wasn't sure how to interpret his expression, and then he laughed again. "You make me fucking crazy, Harlow."

He kissed me swiftly and then rolled us over, somehow managing to lift me into his arms as he stood from the couch. Without even asking, he carried me up the stairs and straight into the shower.

————

Wrapped in Max's strong embrace, I experienced a flicker of anxiety as I was drifting off. I was too comfortable, this felt too good. It couldn't last.

Max's words—telling me this was something that couldn't be ignored, that this was powerful—while true, were vague. I was so prone to looking into meanings that weren't there, because what we were really speaking about was the chemistry between us. That was just sex.

I needed to remember that. I needed to remind my brain and my oh-so-wishful heart that I couldn't expect it to be anything more. That moment of anxiety was brief, if only for the fact that I was simply too content. I felt held and protected in Max's arms.

He was like my own personal heater. I had a tendency to get cold during the night, but I was warm and toasty with his hot, muscled body curled around me. I woke in the darkness at some point, deep in the night, with his hands mapping their way over my body—one sliding over the curve of my belly, the other cupping my breast, his thumb lazily stroking across my puckered nipple.

I didn't even know if he was actually awake. His arousal was pressed against my bottom, and I reflexively arched back into it. If he hadn't been awake, he was in that moment.

I wanted to say we made love. But I didn't want to pin that wishful of a word on what happened. Not just yet.

Be that as it may, it was a slow, sleepy, sensual fucking, with him sinking in from behind me, spooning me while he rocked into me. Pleasure fractured me from the inside out, and I fell asleep only moments after crying out his name.

Chapter Twenty-Four

HARLOW

Waking the following morning, early, as I usually did, I reluctantly slipped out of bed. I didn't want to leave Max's side, but it felt too intimate. I felt as if I were almost being hypnotized, stealthily tumbling headlong into lust and love with him. And most certainly misunderstanding what he might feel for me in the process.

I managed to tiptoe out of the room without waking him. After a quick shower, I tugged on a pair of sweatpants and a soft fleece top and headed downstairs. I started coffee and walked to the windows to look outside into the wintry landscape.

It was still snowing, although it had slowed considerably. It looked as if we'd gotten a good two feet of snowfall since we'd come home last night. Even though I was fairly practical when it came to functioning in the snow, I would've hazarded a guess that even long-time Alaskans were slowed down a bit this morning.

The snow had lightened just enough for me to see the sun hinting at its rise above the mountains in the distance, but it would be another hour or so before light began to claim the darkness. The sky was barely stained pink, with a hint of lavender blending into the fading night sky. I'd grown to love winter sunrises and sunsets. The time felt almost ethereal.

Glancing at the clock mounted in the center of the kitchen wall, I saw it was only seven a.m. and wondered when Max would get up. I knew Ivy was an early riser, and I needed some friend advice. I decided to chance it and call her. If Max woke while we were on the phone, I would have time to end the call.

Once the coffee was ready, I filled a mug, added a dash of cream, and called my best friend. With my feet hooked around the legs of the stool by the counter island, I listened to the phone ring and hoped she would answer.

"Hey!" Ivy said. "What are you calling so early for? Not that I mind. I'm up and so is Owen. I'm in the kitchen working. He's downstairs because he wanted the big screens for some design work. Either you're calling because it's convenient, or you need to talk."

"Good morning. What makes you say that?"

Ivy laughed softly. "Because when you're stressed about something, you call in the morning. What's up?"

Ivy knew me that well. I was relieved she couldn't see me blushing. I didn't mind that she could essentially read me like a book, but it was almost an anticipatory blush for what I was about to tell her.

"Okay, fine. You might be right. I'm calling about Max."

"What about Max? Don't let me forget, my reconnaissance snooping came up with a few details. You first, though."

I was dying to insist she tell me what she knew, but it wasn't going to change the fact that I desperately needed her advice. I jumped in. "I ran into Max in Anchorage after *you* told him I happened to be in town."

Ivy laughed. "How is that a problem?"

"It's not, but, well, we kind of had another night."

"Kind of?"

"The weather was bad, and we were at the same hotel."

"Okay, so you had sex," Ivy said flatly. "And?"

"Well, now he's here, and it's been two nights, and he's saying things that I want to hear, and it's a *really* bad idea. Please remind me that I need to *not* be stupid again." My words tumbled out in a mostly run-on sentence, with anxiety blooming in my chest. I took a gulp of coffee and willed my nerves to settle.

Ivy's sigh filtered through the phone. "Oh sweetie, I'm not gonna tell you not to be stupid again. You weren't stupid before, and I hate when you talk about yourself like that. I think you should give Max a shot."

This time, it was my turn to sigh. "Um, okay. You're all about this thing with Max. Everything I know about him tells me it's not smart. You might as well cut to the chase with whatever you learned."

"I point-blank asked Owen how come Max is never serious with anyone. It's nothing major. But he had a college sweetheart, and things were pretty serious, and then she dumped him. Owen said Max hardly ever talked about it, except one time when he got kind of drunk. Apparently, he bitched about how it turned out the woman only wanted him if he was going to get a high price job at a firm right out of MIT. I guess things kind of went sideways after he took her home to visit his family. Like I said, nothing horrible, but enough to make him cynical, I suppose," Ivy explained.

A shaft of anger pierced me. I was unaccountably protective of Max and angry with this woman who I didn't even know. What an idiot. Whatever I thought about Max, he was a decent man. Somehow, thinking about him being younger and probably more idealistic—like we all are when we're younger—and having someone be that opportunistic about him, infuriated me.

"Oh, and then she tried to get back together with him

after his company started doing really well," Ivy added, her tone derisive.

While she and Owen were quite wealthy, money wasn't something Ivy cared much about. It was almost an afterthought for Owen. I didn't doubt that no matter what happened for them, they would be together for better or worse, richer or poor, and all that jazz. My heart wanted that kind of love, but I just didn't know if it was in the cards for me.

"Well, that sucks," I finally said.

"It does. That's why I think Max just needs the right woman. Owen says Max has never asked him questions about any woman other than you. He thinks the only reason he asked was because we're friends. Do me a favor and give him a chance. I suppose I'm asking *you* to give yourself a chance," she said.

If only it were that simple.

Chapter Twenty-Five

MAX

The muted sound of Harlow's voice woke me, and I smiled. The sheets were cool, leading me to believe she had gotten up earlier. Well, obviously she had. My last memory was of being buried inside of her in the blurry hours of the night. I couldn't say if I had started it, or she had, or if we'd teased each other in our sleep.

Kicking the sheets back, I swung my feet to the floor and stood. Glancing around, my eyes landed on my bag by the dresser. First things first, I needed a shower. As I stepped out of her bedroom, I heard her voice drifting up over the loft railing.

"You know what happened last time, Ivy. I was devastated. I can't put myself through that again."

I paused, almost frozen in the doorway. Never in my life had I actually wanted to eavesdrop, but I found myself standing still and holding my breath, wondering who and what she was talking about and what she might say next. There was a pause, and I gathered Ivy was replying.

"I know, but I have a knack for finding men that aren't emotionally available," Harlow replied to whatever Ivy had said on the other end. "I'm finally doing better. Except for Max, I haven't made any stupid decisions in two years."

It chafed hearing that she considered me a stupid decision. I didn't like it. At all. Nor did I like hearing the pain in her voice when she spoke of whatever had happened before. I knew I couldn't hide up here forever, so I swung the door, ensuring it bumped lightly on the wall and alerted her to my presence.

Striding to the shower, all I could think was that I was going to prove to Harlow that we *weren't* a stupid decision. Any doubts that I previously had, any hesitations about diving into this with her, had gone up in smoke. Though the chemistry between us was enough to burn a damn house down, I knew it wasn't just that. I couldn't imagine *not* having Harlow in my life. That wasn't an option.

I suppose what set it off was the fact that I wasn't worried about any of the logistics. She lived in Alaska, I lived in San Francisco, and our lives were far apart. Yet, somehow our respective best friends were together. I didn't know how it would play out, but either I would come here, or she would come there. I didn't even care about the end result. All I cared about was Harlow.

After a quick shower and pulling on jeans and a shirt, I headed downstairs. Harlow had finished her call with Ivy and was making pancakes. She must not have woken much earlier than me because her hair was still drying. With her dark locks tumbling around her shoulders and her pink cheeks, I wanted to bend her over the counter and take her right then and there. But I shackled my need. That wasn't the way to start today. I sensed she had an easy out if I let her believe this was all about sex.

She glanced up with a smile, a hint of vulnerability flickering in her eyes. Rounding the counter, I leaned over as she flipped a pancake, pressing my lips to her cheek.

"Good morning. You didn't have to make pancakes."

Her eyes caught mine as she turned the burner down.

"We need to eat, and I love to cook. Coffee is ready," she said, gesturing over her shoulder. "I have a lot of shoveling to do. You don't..."

Oh, hell no. That *I* needed to be a *we* in that sentence. "Don't even try to tell me I don't need to help. I'm glad to. When does your driveway get plowed?" I asked, recalling she'd mentioned last night she expected her plow guy to come during the night.

"Looks like he came during the night, but it kept snowing. I'm sure he'll be by again today."

"It's still snowing," I commented with a laugh, as I poured some coffee and glanced to the windows.

"Do you need any cream?" she asked as I took a sip.

"Nope, I like my coffee black."

Rounding to the opposite side of the island where the stove was, I slipped onto a stool and watched as she finished the pancakes.

After a delicious breakfast, a round of shoveling, and the plow guy coming by to clear her drive, Harlow insisted we should go into town for lunch. I was happy to go along with whatever she wanted. I'd taken a little time to check online to zap some work emails about personnel matters and loop Owen in on some of the project issues with the new company.

It wasn't a surprise, but a few of the engineers had tendered their resignations and were being territorial about the designs and patents. With this particular company, the prior owners had done a decent job of preparing staff for the transition, but it didn't mean people weren't cranky about things.

Harlow drove us into town, pulling up in front of what appeared to be a cute little café with a colorful sign that said Firehouse Café. Glancing to me, she said, "This is one of my favorite places here. It's in the original firehouse for the town. She has amazing sandwiches and delicious coffee. After all that shoveling, I'm starving."

Following her inside, I glanced around. What I assumed was once the garage had been transformed into a seating area for the café. The concrete floor had been stained a soft blue, the old fire pole was painted with bright flowers, and the windowsills were pink, with a variety of artwork on the walls. Holiday lights were strung about the windows, the fire pole, and even fashioned into a few stars on the walls. It was a rather cheery place.

Harlow slipped her hand through my elbow, stiffening when she realized what she had done. She started to pull it back, but I caught it with my hand. "Going to try to pretend we're not together this morning?" I teased.

She looked at me, a smile tugging at the corners of her mouth and her cheeks flushing before her gaze sobered quickly. It was as if a shadow had fallen across her. If we had been anywhere other than a public place, I would've asked her if she was okay. I almost kissed her, right then and there, but then someone called her name and she turned away.

"Harlow! So good to see you, dear. I'm sorry I wasn't here when you two dropped off the supplies yesterday. You got everything I needed and then some, so thank you."

The woman speaking came out from behind the counter. The seating in the café was to one side, with a counter and an open kitchen to the other. The woman had dark hair streaked with silver, twisted into a braid. She was round and warm and motherly. Her brown gaze landed on me curiously as she approached us.

"No problem," Harlow said. She glanced at me. "This is Max, he's..."

"Her boyfriend," I said, finishing her sentence and holding my hand out to the woman.

The woman's eyes crinkled at the corners with her smile. "Janet," she said, firmly giving my hand a shake. Her gaze shifted to Harlow. "Well, it looks like you've been keeping secrets."

Harlow's cheeks went pink, and she shook her head. I

imagined if I weren't there, she would be downplaying this. I'd decided to take the direct approach with her. I meant everything I said, and I hoped like hell it would wear down the walls of her resistance eventually. I didn't know everything that lay behind her wariness, but I knew she was well-fortified.

"We're starving," Harlow announced, electing not to reply to Janet's comment. "We shoveled last night and then again this morning."

Janet chuckled as she gestured toward a table by the windows and started walking in that direction. "Oh, I know all about shoveling. I prefer to keep the storms under a foot. Any more than that, and I need help with shoveling at home and here."

Janet seated us at a table by the windows with a clear view of Main Street, which was busy with cars and people walking along the sidewalks.

"I know Harlow's favorite coffee, but what can I get you?" Janet asked.

"As long as it's strong, I'll take the house coffee, straight black."

"Coming right up. Take a look at the menu, and I'll get your order when I come back in a few minutes."

After Janet returned with our coffees, she chatted about a few things while she took our orders. "You know, Ward mentioned that some guy you used to work with in Montana applied for a position on one of the crews here. Any idea who that is? I told him if it's an old friend of yours, I'm sure he's a good guy," Janet said conversationally as I flipped through the menu after Harlow had ordered.

I looked up in time to see Harlow's face had gone pale. "You don't happen to know his name, do you?"

"Sure, some guy named Cliff."

If I thought Harlow's expression had been pale before, it was stark white now. Her eyes shuttered, and her features went tense. Janet turned away momentarily, distracted by someone asking her something from a table nearby. When she turned back, I ordered a salmon burger and waited until Janet was well out of earshot, on her way to the kitchen.

I'd told myself I would try to keep things light today, but I couldn't take the pain in Harlow's eyes.

"Are you okay?"

Max's question was expected, yet when I looked into his eyes and sensed he could see how emotionally rattled I was, anxiety spun in my chest, tightening around my heart like a vise. I would've given anything to tell him what was going on inside, for him to tell me Cliff was a jerk and that I had made it through to the other side. I needed reassurance. I needed to lean on someone.

But I had to lean on myself. Not that I needed anything else to give me a blindingly obvious reminder of how alone I was in the world. Hearing that Cliff was trying to transfer here to one of the hotshot crews was a brutally painful reminder. I could *not* expect anyone else to be there for me. Whenever I did that, the consequences were disastrous for my emotional sanity.

"I'm fine. It's just kind of weird to hear about that guy," I belatedly replied.

Max stared at me, his gaze far more perceptive than I preferred. "What's weird about it?" he asked.

I sensed he was being careful and concerned about how I might respond, and that bothered me. I didn't need anyone reading into me. What I said next surprised me. I suppose, in hindsight, it was pure reaction. I was brutally honest.

"Well, I guess it's weird because we used to date. Or, I guess I should say, I *thought* we were dating. Until I found out he was fucking two other women at the same time. I didn't find that out until after I got pregnant and had a miscarriage."

My words landed like a rock on the table between us. Max's eyes widened slightly, and then narrowed.

"What?" he asked, his tone low.

I had never seen Max angry, but I felt certain he was furious right now, and I wanted to cry. I was well over Cliff, but it didn't change how emotionally traumatic the miscarriage had been. I'd gotten my feelings all tangled up into this crazy, wishful idea of a happily-ever-after package that didn't exist. It had been an unplanned pregnancy, and then I pinned a bunch of hopes on it, thinking something could come of it. No matter how much of an ass Cliff had turned out to be, I had wanted things to work at the time.

More than anything, all my life, I had craved stability and someone to love me. I recalled my therapist's words: *"That's an inside job."* I also recalled her pointing out that while many children didn't get what they needed from their parents, it didn't change the fact that they had to figure it out on their own as adults. Life wasn't fair, and the world didn't owe anyone anything.

My therapist hadn't said that last part, she was kinder than that, but it was the truth and something I reminded myself of often. I couldn't bank on anyone being there for me.

As I looked over at Max and saw the anger in his eyes, I wished I could trick myself again and hope for something that would never be.

"He's a fucking asshole," Max said flatly. I hadn't gotten

around to answering his vague *what* question, but it didn't really matter.

"Well, yeah, and I'm the idiot who got involved with him," I replied, weariness rolling through me.

Max reached over, catching my hand in his, his grip warm, strong, and sure.

"You're not the idiot. No one's an idiot for trusting other people. People do shitty things. It's not the fault of the people on the other end. Please tell me you're going to let Ward know he shouldn't even consider this guy."

"Max, I can't tell Ward who to hire," I protested.

"Fair enough, but you can tell him this guy's a fucking asshole. That has nothing to do with you. Anyone who treats you like that is an dick and doesn't deserve a chance to weasel his way back into your life."

"Max, it wasn't like my pregnancy was planned. In fact, that pregnancy is why I stopped taking the pill and switched to an IUD. When I'm out in the field, my schedule is a little nuts. I'm not saying Cliff's a good guy. I'm just saying..."

My words ran out because I didn't know quite what to say. The idea of Cliff working anywhere near me stressed me right the hell out. Not because I still carried any feelings for him, but because of what he represented and his link to a very painful time in my life.

"Lots of us don't plan on things that happen. That's not a license to screw around with two people and leave you to deal with a miscarriage on your own. That's what happened, right?" he asked, his eyes fierce.

Nodding, I swallowed through the tightness in my throat. Hearing it spelled out so plainly stung a little. It was like the scab over an old wound had been torn open. I *was* okay, but this was a painful reminder of how *not* okay I'd been in the aftermath of that.

I felt as if Max was willing me to hear him. All I knew was I was suddenly overwhelmed emotionally, and I didn't want to try to process any of this in the middle of downtown Willow Brook.

"I'll let Ward know things didn't end on a good note, but that's it. I don't want everyone to know what went down. I'm sorry I dumped that on you. I was shocked when Janet told me he'd applied here, and I wasn't really thinking," I explained.

Max was quiet, his gaze considering. I didn't know what he was thinking, and I had so many questions. A motion caught my eye, and I looked over to see Janet threading through the tables with our food. Her interruption was welcome, if only because it automatically changed the subject.

As we were walking out a little while later, Max reached for my hand, glancing down. "I know you think you've pegged me, but you haven't. You didn't deserve what that asshole did. I'm not sure what you're thinking, but don't write us off."

―――――

Though the reason for the crew schedules getting rearranged made perfect sense, a part of me wished my crew was on duty for local calls this week. When winter rolled around, we mostly handled local calls. For obvious reasons, what with the landscape being blanketed in snow, fires in the backcountry died down in the winter. We handled occasional controlled burns because early and late winter offered good conditions for that. Otherwise, the three hotshot crews housed out of Willow Brook Fire & Rescue took turns covering local calls, both in town and the surrounding area.

Max's unexpected visit had sent me spinning inside. My emotions were all over the map, and I couldn't get purchase inside. It would've been nice to shoo him away because I had to work. Part of me wished he hadn't been present when Ward told me I was off for the week because I could've come up with some sort of excuse. I couldn't bring myself to lie though, and didn't enjoy feeling like a coward. There was also the very unsettling fact that I *loved* having him around. A bit too much.

The following morning, I was up even earlier than usual. I would've liked to have said it was because I wanted to get out of bed. But no. I had to pee. I'd woken warm against Max's side, my calf thrown over his, with my head tucked into his shoulder. His arm was curled around me, holding me close.

Even in rest, he was hard and muscled. I did *not* want to get out of bed. At all. But my body had some thoughts about that. In my mind, once awake, I was frantically doing gymnastics, trying to pull my wishful heart away from the ledge. I was falling headlong into everything I felt for Max and needed to save myself.

Even though the clock read five thirty a.m. in bright blue numbers, I carefully untangled myself, slipped out from under the covers, and tiptoed out of the room. The temptation to return to bed was strong. As an act of resistance, I climbed into the shower instead. With the steaming water pouring over me, I contemplated that I was staring down into the abyss of another heartbreak. I couldn't quite believe I had allowed this to happen.

After we had lunch at Firehouse Café yesterday afternoon, and I'd blurted out the truth about Cliff, we took care of a few errands before returning home. Restless and needing something to do, I had made dinner. That mundane task had stitched me closer and closer to Max. Growing up bouncing between hotels meant I hadn't had evenings at home for most of my childhood after my mother passed away. As a result, something as simple as dinner at home with someone was fraught with meaning for me.

I couldn't quite believe Max was trying to tell me to give us a chance, and not to write us off, because the reality was, our lives didn't mesh. I was here in Willow Brook, and he ran a corporation three thousand miles away.

But he's here now. He also has a reason to come to Alaska now. You don't have to stay here. It would be worth it to make some changes to be with Max.

See? There went my wishful thoughts, off to the races. My heart was so desperate. It wasn't helping to spend so much time with Max, it only made me like him more. The sex alone was enough to make me fall for him. Hell, the man could practically make me come with nothing more than a hot look.

With a hard shake of my head, a rather futile attempt to shut up my wishful mind and heart, I reached for the conditioner. As I ran my hands through my hair, I remembered last night with Max's hand lacing into my hair as he buried himself inside of me. I blushed all over simply thinking about it.

Hurrying out of the shower, I tugged on a pair of leggings and a long-sleeved T-shirt. All the while, I was trying to come up with an excuse for why Max needed to leave.

But you don't want him to leave. More than that, you need to stop being stupid.

Every time I thought about him leaving, it was like a paper cut over the surface of my heart. The pain was small, but sharp. As I replayed our conversation at Firehouse Café, I started coffee. My thoughts spun back to Janet's comment about Cliff. What the hell was he doing?

Cliff knew I had taken a position here. I couldn't imagine what he was thinking.

I'd fallen for Cliff hard during my hotshot training. When I found out I was pregnant, I was shocked at first, and then I spun fantasies around it. As I usually did, because I was always looking high and low for love; I'd read into things that weren't even happening. In hindsight, it was quite obvious. Cliff never made any promises. It was all just my own wishful thinking.

Even though I certainly hadn't planned to get pregnant, I had wanted my baby. So badly. Everything was all tangled up together. My doctor said after the fact that she couldn't give me a definitive reason why I miscarried. I had a fall out in the field and lost the baby a few days later. Whether it was a result of that fall, I'd never know.

All of this and more illuminated why I needed to be careful about where my thoughts went when it came to Max. Not because I had any intention of getting pregnant. Rather, I needed to keep my heart from becoming vulnerable. I needed guarantees that weren't fair to ask of anyone.

The sound of Max's feet hitting the floor upstairs reached me, and I quickly spun away from the windows. It was just past six now, and the sun still wouldn't be up for a while. Night was gradually fading into dawn, but light had yet to claim the darkness.

Once I heard the shower turn on, I went to the refrigerator to assess what to make for breakfast. I settled on omelets and began pulling out the ingredients. I was whisking eggs a few minutes later, when Max came downstairs.

When I glanced up, he was walking toward me. His dark hair was damp from the shower and his blue eyes were bright. With the shadow of stubble on his jaw, he was even more handsome than usual. My mind flashed to the feel of those whiskers on the insides of my thighs last night when he sent me flying with his mouth and his fingers.

My heart gave a hard thump, a swift kick against my ribs. Emotion hit me in a wave. I was in a freefall with him, and didn't know how to stop it.

Chapter Twenty-Seven

MAX

Later that afternoon, my phone buzzed on the table. Spinning it around, I saw Owen's name flash on the screen and considered whether to answer right now. Harlow had announced she needed to go into the grocery store. Though I had wanted to go with her, I needed do some work online.

While it was true I could do a lot of what needed to be done from a distance, this company acquisition was fresh, so it called for my focus. I also needed to get caught up on emails related to a few matters at headquarters in San Francisco. As such, I was situated on a stool at the island in the kitchen with a cup of coffee, and a fire in the woodstove. Figuring there was no reason not to take the call, I tapped the screen, answering by speaker.

"Hey man, what's up?"

"Hey, I was just calling to ask the same of you. I was talking to the lead engineer on one of the projects, and she mentioned you're not in Anchorage. Did I miss something?" Owen asked.

I chuckled, realizing I hadn't bothered to let Owen know

I was taking off for a few days. I knew it would lead to questions, but I figured I might as well fill him in.

"Oh, and Ivy mentioned you're at Harlow's place in Willow Brook. She's asking me questions about your past and how come you've never been serious with anyone. She also told me I would be responsible for kicking your ass if you hurt Harlow," Owen added with a wry chuckle.

"I see."

"You planning to let me know what the hell is going on?"

I ran a hand through my hair with a sigh and took a sip of coffee. "Of course. I suppose I should've updated you that I was going to run things from a distance for a few days. I ran into Harlow in Anchorage at the hotel, and now I'm here."

"I think we've covered that part, although now I know how you ended up there. Ivy *will* kick your ass if you hurt Harlow, so I'm wondering if that's something she needs to worry about." I could practically feel Owen's eye roll through the phone line.

"Look, maybe it's crazy, but Harlow means something to me. I know I probably need to get back to Anchorage. The timing for me to be gone more than a day or two isn't great."

"It's not a big deal. If you need me to, I can head up there. I was only calling because we have a small mutiny with two of the engineers." Owen didn't push me on Harlow, which was a relief for the moment. I was still muddling through my own feelings and not quite in a place to explain them. He continued, "You know how we set up the computer monitoring for the internal systems?"

"Yeah. Like we always do. What's happening?"

"One of them was trying to download the patented designs offsite. It wasn't possible because of the firewall, but I called up there this morning when I checked the alerts. Honestly, I think we should both meet there to deal with this. It sounds like it's not great timing for you, and I'm sorry. How about we meet there tomorrow, and then I'll stay? You can head back to Willow Brook once we resolve this."

"Fuck," I muttered. "There's always something. It's a good engineer team. I don't like to see them pulling this kind of bullshit."

"Of course not, but better now than later. We've got two problem staff to deal with. The rest probably need a morale boost, and a reminder that if we hadn't bought out the company, it was on the way to going under. So we'll meet there tomorrow then?"

Owen didn't waste much time when it came to problem-solving. He preferred to address issues head-on. Beyond our long friendship, that was another factor that made it easy for us to work together. We had similar styles and weren't much for endless planning meetings.

"Yeah, I can be there in the morning. Do you need me to pick you up at the airport?"

"No, I'll drive. I have a list of things Ivy would like me to pick up for the holidays. Want to fill me in on what's going on with Harlow? I told Ivy that there was no way you would hurt Harlow on purpose, but I've never known you to be serious, not since grad school."

Owen knew what had happened with my last serious relationship. We didn't speak of it much because there wasn't much else to say. In hindsight, I wasn't too broken up about it, although I had loved Cheryl in the only way I knew how at that age. More than anything, it had been a wake-up call about keeping my eyes on what mattered. At the time, that had been my fledgling business.

Harlow had spun everything on its axis, landing me on a different continent, relationship-wise. I considered what to say to Owen, opting for the simplest and most brutally honest explanation.

"Harlow's different. Tease me if you want, but I want something with her. The only problem is, I'm not so sure she wants the same thing."

Owen was quiet long enough that I deduced I'd startled him. "You there?"

He chuckled. "Oh, I'm here. Just didn't quite expect that. I'm the first to argue that finding the right woman is the best thing ever. I wouldn't give up Ivy for anything. Of all the things you don't need to worry about with Harlow, you certainly don't need to worry about her wanting you for your money. Her father cut her off, and she didn't even care."

His comment was an oblique reference to my ex. Of course, my ex hadn't had the sense to look at the long-term, but by then, it didn't matter anymore. I was damn relieved she'd shown her true colors early on.

"I know. I always said Howard May was a fucking asshole. The way he treats Harlow is bullshit. She's his fucking daughter. It's not about the money, but I can't believe he cut her off just because she refused to work with him," I said.

"Totally agree with you there."

Taking a deep breath, I decided to go straight to the heart of what had been spinning through my thoughts. I wasn't much for asking for advice, but Owen was one of the few friends I turned to. "I've got a question for you."

"What's that?"

"Any suggestions on how to persuade Harlow this is worth it?"

Owen laughed softly. "Damn. Never thought anyone would come to me for relationship advice."

"Yeah, well, I never thought I'd be asking."

"For starters, I think you need to be clear on what you mean by *this*," Owen explained.

"Look, man, I'm in love with her. That's what I mean by *this*."

I think I stunned him into silence, although I'd done the same to myself. It wasn't as if I hadn't realized Harlow meant a lot to me. Yet, the ease with which that word slipped out was shocking.

"What the hell? Don't take this the wrong way, but don't you think things are moving a little quickly? If my math is right, it's only been a few days," Owen finally said.

A flash of defensiveness rose inside. "No, it's been over a year. When you two threw us together at your place last year, well, let's just say, something happened. It might have been only one night, but I never forgot. I'm getting some sense of why trust doesn't come easy to her, but that's my biggest roadblock right now."

"Damn, you know how to keep things quiet," Owen muttered. "I think you're just gonna have to show her. I don't have any great relationship advice. I'm still pretty sure the only reason Ivy's with me is because she didn't have enough sense to tell me no."

At that, I laughed. I had said something along that variation many times to tease him. "Maybe it's true, but I'm pretty sure she loves you too. Do me a favor...ask Ivy."

Owen's laugh rumbled through the line. "Will do. I suppose I can assure her she doesn't need to worry about you breaking Harlow's heart."

"Hell no."

Chapter Twenty-Eight

MAX

Later that evening, I took a pull of my beer and glanced across the counter at Harlow. She was in the midst of chopping onions for a stir-fry she was making. She clearly liked to cook, and I finally decided to ask a question that had been feathering through my thoughts every so often.

"So tell me, with your dad traveling all over the place and taking you with him when you were growing up, when did you learn to cook?"

Harlow's wide brown eyes met mine, a flicker of sadness in them. It passed quickly. She lifted the cutting board and carefully used the knife to slide the onions into a pan.

"Before my mother died, I used to spend time with her in the kitchen. I was pretty young, so I didn't learn too much, but she loved cooking. Later, one of my nannies got me this mini oven-stove thing, something I could use in a hotel. She knew I loved to cook and bake, so she taught me a few things. Then, I went off to college and it was a bit of trial by fire. I guess I sort of taught myself. If I ever build my own place, the most important room will be the kitchen. I know how I would want it set up and everything," she said with a little laugh, her cheeks staining pink.

I fucking hated hearing how lonely her childhood must've been. My own childhood stood out in stark contrast. My parents had their noses in everything I did, much to my chagrin when I was a teenager. My mother had actually insisted I learn to cook because she didn't want her son to turn out to be a man who couldn't cook a good meal for himself, or someone he loved. Her words, not mine.

I wanted to give Harlow everything she wanted. That meant I needed to figure out a way for my life to be a little more settled. I didn't travel quite as much as I used to, now that my company was well-established, but I still traveled some. I didn't know if Harlow had strong feelings about where she lived. I did know I was bound and determined to figure something out that meant we could be together.

My mind turned to the next matter at hand. I needed to let her know I would be leaving tomorrow for a day or two, and I wasn't sure how she was going to react.

"By the way, I have to head into Anchorage tomorrow. We have a personnel issue to deal with, and Owen's meeting me there."

Harlow's eyes flicked to mine from where she was adjusting the heat on the burner under the onions. Her expression was carefully bland, and I didn't like it. Even though we had only spent a few days together, I had come to learn she was quite expressive, her face an open book, when her guard was down. When her mask was firmly in place, her expression went almost blank, like this. I wanted to shake her fucking father and beat the crap out of every man who had hurt her since then.

"Okay. It's not like I expected you to stay," she finally said, her words measured.

"I'll be back in a few days. You can count on it," I said flatly.

Harlow stared at me, her hand pausing in the motion of

stirring and then picking up again as she looked away. "Max, I don't have any expectations."

Oh, hell no. I was *not* going to allow the conversation to go in this direction. I slipped off the stool and rounded the counter. Wrapping my arms around her waist from behind, I could feel the tension vibrating through her body.

"Harlow, maybe I wasn't planning on this, but I'm not going anywhere. Where I might be geographically doesn't change a thing with us. Anchorage is only forty-five minutes away, when the weather's good at least. Don't you dare go thinking I'm going to drive away and that's the end of us."

I felt her breath hitch. She stirred the onions again and then turned the burner off, setting the spatula on the counter. She didn't turn in my arms, though, and held herself still. When I heard her take a shaky breath, I realized she was crying, or at least on the verge of tears.

"Harlow, look at me," I murmured into her hair, my heart squeezing so hard it hurt.

Her hands curled around the edge of the counter as if she needed something to hold onto. Her knuckles went white with her grip. "Max, you can't do this. I can't do this."

Rather than trying to push the issue, I tucked my head into the crook of her neck and simply held her. She took several shaky breaths, each one tightening the fist clenched around my heart.

If you had told me I was going to fall for Harlow, for any woman, so thoroughly that I wouldn't even think twice about it, I would've laughed long and hard. A single night with her, over a year ago now, had scared the hell out of me. I knew now that I hadn't quite been ready at the time to face the emotion only Harlow could elicit. She stirred deep waters. She reminded me what I could have, the very thing I'd told myself wasn't worth fighting for, once upon a time.

Now, I knew so completely what she meant that I had cast aside any logical, rational arguments to make against it.

There was no way in hell I wasn't going to fight for this, for *us*, for *her*.

It fucking slayed me to sense even a glimmer of the pain she felt. I didn't know everything in her heart. I certainly hadn't pieced together all of her past. I really only knew she had lost her mother when she was young and had grown up with an emotionally absent father who had been the opposite of supportive to her.

I couldn't even imagine Harlow trying to work with her father, not with the way he worked. Then, to hear what had happened with Cliff—or rather, the *fucking asshole*, as I'd come to call him in my mind—had likely served to rub salt in the open wounds left behind by her father's emotional neglect.

Those bits and pieces of information helped me understand why she was so guarded, but I was still flying blind. Once upon a time, I would've thought I could pick my way through the rubble of this. Yet, everything paled in comparison to the depth of what I felt for Harlow. Nothing even came close. Harlow had shown me that you couldn't know what love was until something was on the line.

I had to get this right. I took it as a win that Harlow didn't shove me away, and her breath slowly evened. I lifted my head, breathing her in. I had one hand curled around her waist, my palm splayed over her belly. I could feel every breath she took and the subtle thud of her heartbeat echoing through her body.

Lifting my other hand, I brushed her hair away from her face, pressing a kiss to her temple. Eventually, the tension eased in her body, and her grip loosened on the edge of the counter. Only then did I speak.

"I didn't plan on this, on *us*. If I'd had a little more courage last year, I wouldn't have left." I could sense she was listening, so I kept going. "Before you start worrying, I didn't make up my reason for leaving last year. There *was* an urgent business meeting, and I needed to be there. It's just that it gave me an easy out. Maybe you don't want to say it yet, but I knew that night that this thing between us wasn't just lust."

I paused, considering my words carefully. "It's not. I know it, and I know you know it too. I'm not going to pretend I understand everything that's going on with you because I don't. But I think I'm getting an idea why you think we can't do this. Or rather, why you think *you* can't do it."

I waited, trying to gauge how she might be responding with nothing but the feel of her body in my arms to go on. "I'm not going anywhere, Harlow. I don't give up. I sure as hell won't give up on us."

Harlow finally turned in my arms. Her cheeks were damp with tears, and her eyes glistened. The look in her gaze nearly killed me—so raw and so vulnerable. As I watched, she shuttered her gaze. It was as if she was battening down the hatches around herself inside.

"Max, you can't know how this is going to go. I'm already in too deep. You don't even live here. This is... I don't know, a little island floating outside of your actual life. Don't..."

Anger pierced me. Not anger with Harlow, but anger at every event and every person in her life who had boxed her in like this. It was as if she felt like she couldn't believe in something. When I shook my head sharply, her words trailed off.

"Don't tell me that. I can run my company from anywhere. Hell, when my best friend is here in Alaska doing pretty much what I do, I can do the same. I don't care about the details. We'll figure it out."

Emotion hit me hard, and I dipped my head because words weren't enough. I fit my mouth over hers and poured everything into our kiss. Cupping her face with my hands, I swept my tongue inside the warm sweetness of her mouth, moaning when her tongue tangled with mine. On a gasp, she arched into me and kissed me back, just as hard and rough.

A soft cry escaped her throat when I drew back. Another

J.H. CROIX

tear rolled down her cheek, and I wiped it away with my thumb, never once looking away.

I certainly didn't know everything, but I knew one thing with absolute faith. I loved Harlow, and I would fight for her.

"I love you, you know."

Her eyes widened, pure terror entering her gaze. She shook her head rapidly, her breath coming in shuddering gasps. "You can't know that, Max. It's too soon."

"I know what I feel, and this feels right. Just trust me."

As soon as those last three words slipped from my lips, I realized I couldn't have chosen a worse thing to say to her. Life had not given her many reasons to trust men, if any.

She surprised me by remaining still, and simply holding my gaze. I wished I could climb inside of her mind and disprove every shouting doubt. I practically held my breath, and then she lifted a hand, placing it on my chest, right over my heart.

"I think sex is on your brain. You're confusing that with love. Go to Anchorage tomorrow."

Chapter Twenty-Nine

HARLOW

Sitting across the table, I looked over at Maisie, who was holding her toddler, Max, on her lap. He was a cute little boy, with Maisie's curly dark hair, and was all wiggles. My heart squeezed a little, and I looked away. His presence was a dual whammy for me—he shared Max's name, and his existence was a reminder of the child I didn't have.

"I've gained twenty pounds," Lucy announced, as she laid a card on the table.

Susannah, who sat at an angle across from her, laughed and shook her head. "Well, I gained almost forty while I was pregnant. So count yourself lucky if twenty is your max."

Lucy rolled her eyes and took a sip of her water. Maisie was hosting card night at the home she shared with Beck, and had invited me to come. Beck was out with the guys. Their younger daughter, Carol, was sound asleep in her crib upstairs. Maisie had a handy baby monitor sitting in the center of the table. Thus far, all we'd heard was the steady sound of baby Carol's breathing and a few gurgles.

Little Max hadn't been so amenable to going to bed,

though he looked as if he was about to drop off to sleep as he struggled to keep his eyes open. Meanwhile, I was having trouble reminding myself that I didn't need to run around wishing for babies every time I encountered a small child.

Apparently, that wasn't an unusual side effect after a miscarriage. Although it seemed to be dragging on for me. I thought it had passed, but lately I was craving babies again. When I'd gone in for my annual gynecological check up—always fun times—my doctor had gently pointed out that I was also approaching the age where my body had biological expectations.

"Biological expectations" seemed a rather dry, impersonal way to explain the emotional bursts I'd been experiencing, but I'd take it.

I presumed she meant that whole biological clock thing. I hadn't wanted to clarify further with her. I suspected being around Max, not babies, was what had stirred me up inside. The same thing had happened last year after our ill-fated one-night stand. The baby cravings had passed and the longing to fall madly in love, and be loved in return, had also faded.

"No way in hell am I gaining forty pounds," Lucy retorted. "I'll be as big as a house then."

Susannah shrugged nonchalantly. "I felt more like a whale than a house."

Maisie chuckled as she stood, adjusting a now sleepy Max in her arms. "I'd say it's more like a beach ball, one that someone could just pop. If only labor was that easy."

Amelia leaned her elbows on the table, her gaze scanning the group. I was curious to know why she didn't have children yet, but then she surprised me by stating, "I guess now is as good a time as any."

"For what?" Ella asked as she snagged a tortilla chip from a bowl in the middle of the table.

"I'm pregnant."

Everybody spoke at once.

"What?!"

"Oh my God, that's so awesome!"

"When did you find out?"

"Is this planned, or an accident?" Lucy asked with a grin, ending the brief cacophony.

Amelia rolled her eyes. "It was planned, but you already knew, so stop being ridiculous."

Lucy shrugged and grinned. "How about *you* gain the forty pounds? I'll stick with twenty. Although you're tall, you're probably hardly going to show."

Conversation drifted around me, most of it about the trials of being pregnant. All the while, I was feeling a little melancholy.

When I left a little bit later, I almost called Ivy on the way home, but decided against it. While she was an early riser, she wasn't much of a late night person. Not that it was too late, but still.

Driving home in the cold, under a gorgeous starry night, I wondered if I could ever have what my newfound friends all appeared to have. Messy lives where they were loved.

Everything Max said the other day had been playing on a loop in my thoughts. It started up again just now, like a record set on repeat. The needle fell and my thoughts spun along the grooves.

Max was teaching me a surprising lesson, something I had never expected. I had craved love for so long. The words he said the other day—about fighting for us, about it taking him by surprise, about how it was worth it—had burrowed into my heart with unerring accuracy. There was a time when I would've given just about anything to hear that. Yet, now I knew, I probably wouldn't have believed it.

I didn't have faith in the vagaries of the universe. I didn't have faith in anyone loving me. Max had said all the right things, and all I had wanted to do was cry. I was simply waiting for him to realize he was crazy.

You're not even giving him a chance. Just like Ivy said. You don't give anyone a chance.

I'd had some variation of this internal debate going on whenever I wasn't entirely occupied. Max had left a few days ago, and I'd completely ignored his texts and calls since. I figured that was easier than seeing the reality on his face when he realized he was confusing lust with love.

The snow crunched under my tires as I turned down my driveway. Rolling to a stop in front of the house, I cut the engine and the quiet settled around me. I climbed out of my little truck, the sound of the door loud in the peaceful night. My footsteps were muted against the packed snow as I walked onto the porch and spun in a slow circle. I didn't know if it was true, but it felt like the stars were actually closer here in Alaska. They looked near enough for me to reach up and touch them. On cold winter nights, they glittered brightly, like diamonds thrown across the sky.

As I looked up into the darkness, there was a shimmer of green in the distance. The Northern Lights appeared every so often, a translucent curtain rippling across the sky. Streaks of dark and light green formed, shimmering as I watched. My heart squeezed, my breath lost in the moment. The wilderness could steal your breath and make you remember that you were nothing but a speck in its massive theater.

I gulped in the crisp, icy air, allowing it to cleanse my lungs, and misting when I exhaled. With one last look at the stars and the sky, just as a raven called through the darkness, I walked inside. I toed my boots off and hung my jacket by the door. In a burst of energy the other day, I had gotten a Christmas tree. I couldn't bear to cut a tree, so I had gotten a small spruce that I could plant next spring. Bright blue lights circled the branches, with a big star on top and nothing else.

I didn't have any plans for Christmas, although Ivy had texted yesterday and invited me to come to Diamond Creek.

I was undecided, but I would probably go if only because I didn't want to be alone.

I started a fire in the woodstove and then flicked on the television, attempting to lose myself in mindless shows. Over and over again, that record started playing in my mind— Max's words and my reaction to them.

Chapter Thirty

MAX

"This is bullshit," I commented, looking at Owen across the table.

My best friend nodded and leaned back in his chair. "Most definitely. We've already put a stop to it, but now we need to decide what to do next."

We were at the headquarters of the small engineering firm we had acquired, meeting privately in the conference room. One of the lead engineers had attempted to essentially steal several of the primary patented designs. We learned about this through our internal monitoring. The other lead engineer had also sent us an email about it.

The team here was strong and capable, staffed with excellent engineers. They had done good work for this company. I completely understood the urge to take ownership of the work. Yet, this guy didn't seem to understand that all of his research and time had been paid for and buttressed by the work of others on his team. The company owned the patents. He didn't seem to have enough sense to realize that if we hadn't stepped in and bought the company out, he'd have been in a much worse position than he was now, with the patents parceled off through the bankruptcy process.

The cascade of events that could have happened would've been substantially worse. In this situation, we had actually offered the engineer the same position, with better pay, if he chose to stay. We would deal with his actions, but it likely meant letting him go.

"We'll talk with him today and explain the options," I said.

Owen nodded. "No need to take any disciplinary action. We can offer him a clean option to walk away and leave it at that. If, and that's a big if, he wants to remain here, we need to have some serious discussions about safeguards and his commitment to our work."

"You want to give him a shot? That is, if he wants to stay."

Owen drummed his fingertips on the table and shrugged. "I don't actually know. I know he's skilled as hell. The work he did before he was at this company speaks for itself. I'm guessing he's just not thinking clearly. He got too hung up on the idea that designs belong to him since he was part of creating them."

I shook my head and chuckled. "I'm guessing Ivy argued to keep him."

Owen threw his head back with a laugh and shrugged. "Of course she did. You know how she is. She's focused only on his engineering and design skills. I did point out that we'd have to put some monitoring in place long-term after he pulled this. But she insisted it's a sign that he's passionate about his work."

Taking a sip of my coffee, I rolled my eyes. "Passionate, huh? It's not that I don't see her point. Let's meet with him together and see what we think afterwards."

This afternoon had been busy. Before I'd left to go stay with Harlow for a few days, I had already set the wheels in motion to get the signage changed on the building and what-not. The workers were here today taking care of that. We had decided to use the name of Owen's company—Off the Grid—on the building, website, and more. Considering that we intended to keep this place based here in Anchorage, it made sense to use a name that was familiar in Alaska. My company would remain listed as a primary owner on all the legal paperwork only, although I would have just as much involvement in running the business.

The patents in question that had led to this personnel scuffle were valuable. They related to battery life for fuel cells, in addition to more efficient methods of wind capture. We wanted them, and we would definitely use them. Unlike the prior owners, between Owen's company and mine, we already had the capacity to put them on the market much sooner than if this company had remained independent.

With workers scattered about the building changing signs, even the admin staff were on edge. Sometimes, I wondered how often management held back on letting staff know how dire the finances were toward the end stages of a company. In this case, it appeared they had given a few clues, but they hadn't let it out that they were staring down bankruptcy within a matter of months. There had been no viable way out at the time. That said, I'd learned over the years that human nature in business tended toward denial. That wasn't to imply people were stupid, just that they hoped for the best, even when it made no sense.

Often, when businesses were glorified in the press, the nitty-gritty details were left out. The dry, often boring, logistics associated with budgeting and long-term planning weren't too sexy when it came to news spreads on startups. With renewable energy all the rage these days—not politically, per se, but socially—cutting edge engineering companies that were trying to make strides in this technology were often in the news. The state of their business, separate from their star projects, was often left out of any news reports.

In short, most of the staff here didn't have all the details on just how dire the situation had been. When I notified the receptionist for the former CEO, who was now technically my receptionist, that we needed to meet with the engineer who had attempted to steal those designs, I thought her eyebrows were about to fly off her forehead.

Owen had taken a call in the executive conference room, so I decided to take a moment to try to set her at ease. Leaning my hip against the desk, I looked over at her.

"Harriet, I promise you don't need to worry about your job. No one here needs to worry about jobs getting cut. Owen and I know transitions like this are challenging. I'm sorry for that. I was under the impression that the former owners had given you a bit more information on the financial status of the company. It wasn't good. In fact, it was so bad, that they were facing bankruptcy within a matter of months. There was no good way out other than for someone else to buy the company."

Harriet, who I had come to learn was a steady, more than competent administrative support person, looked at me quietly. I took it as a good sign that her eyebrows had lowered from her hairline. With her short, curly brown hair and kind blue eyes, she gave off a warm, supportive air. I could only imagine that the naturally expected waves of gossip and emotion associated with the company being sold off had rattled her. Whether it was warranted or not, administrative staff—particularly someone in her position—often ended up at the center of the storm, so to speak, when things like this happened. I would have been willing to bet that some staff thought she knew what was coming, regardless of whether she did or not.

After a moment, she nodded slowly. "People are a little upset. Overall, everyone seems to like you. Bill has been frustrated with the situation. He had a lot of leeway under the former management, and I think he's concerned he won't have the same flexibility going forward. I didn't know everything, but I was aware the company wasn't financially stable. If there's anything I can do to help settle some feathers, please let me know."

For a moment, I considered offering her a raise on the spot. I'd learned over the years as the CEO of my own company that it was damn hard to train attitude and ethics, if not impossible. Harriet had both in spades. Yet, now wasn't the time to casually offer up a raise. Once Owen and I had a better handle on the situation, she'd be on the top of the list.

Pushing my hip off the desk, I nodded. "I appreciate that. I think just doing what you've already been doing is helpful. We'll muddle through this transition. I can assure you the company will stay financially stable going forward. We wouldn't have chosen to purchase the company if we hadn't believed we could stabilize the situation. In the meantime, if you don't mind buzzing Bill down, I'll be in the conference room with Owen."

Harriet smiled. "Of course, I'll have him come down right now."

———

That evening, I leaned back in my chair, at a table in the very bar where I'd seen Harlow less than a week prior. Owen and I had stayed at the corporate offices until it was quite late, reviewing financials and personnel information, along with a deep dive into current projects.

I was relieved to have been legitimately quite busy all day because I had *not* wanted to leave Harlow a few days ago. Harlow had ignored every text and call since, and I fucking hated it. I was torn with what to do about it. I really wanted to storm back to Willow Brook and demand she stop avoiding me. Just as strongly, I suspected she would not appreciate that approach at all.

Owen was finishing a call with Ivy, and I glanced around the restaurant while I waited. The hotel had decorated for

Christmas, with lights strung about the bar, and a small tree on a table in a corner. My mother had called today and asked when I would be flying home. Normally, I would've simply asked her what day was best and made arrangements. Although Ivy had teased about worrying about me over the holidays, my workaholic habits had eased slightly in the last few years. With my company on stable ground now, I had the ability to set the terms for my schedule.

The only hesitation I had about going home was I wanted some sort of resolution with Harlow before I left Alaska. If I had my way, she would come home with me. I didn't like the idea of her being alone over the holidays. Not one bit.

"If all goes well, I should be on the way home tomorrow, or the day after," Owen said, pausing and glancing my way. I presumed Ivy was saying something. "Of course, I'll tell Max. Love you, bye."

Lowering the phone from his ear, Owen set it on the table beside him. I took a swallow of my whiskey, and eyed him. "What do you need to tell Max?" I asked with a wink.

Owen chuckled and took a sip of his drink before replying. "She's hoping you'll come to Diamond Creek for Christmas if you're not going home."

"She'll have to get in line behind my mom."

"So you're heading to Pennsylvania then?"

I shrugged. "I'm not sure. My parents would love to have me there. If I don't make it for Christmas, I'll definitely visit them sometime within the next month."

"If you're not going to Pennsylvania now, then where will you be for Christmas? I'm not asking because I'm nosy. I'm asking because Ivy will ask, and I'd better have the answer."

Draining my whiskey, I set my glass down with a chuckle. "Well, you can tell her I'm hoping to be wherever Harlow happens to be. If Harlow will answer my damn calls."

"What do you mean?"

I hadn't set out to talk about Harlow, but I'd been

mentally spinning my wheels on her for days now and needed someone else's lens on it. "She's been ignoring me. Not replying to texts or calls. I'm considering just showing up at her doorstep, but I'm not so sure she would appreciate that."

Owen arched a brow, his gaze thoughtful. "I know Ivy invited her down to visit with us. Ivy's parents will be at the house, so if Harlow comes, she'll be staying at the lodge."

Our waitress passed by after delivering food to another table, pausing beside us when I caught her eye. I ordered another drink, if only because I needed something to settle my nerves. That was saying something because only Harlow could rattle me like this. I didn't like how out of control I felt.

All she had done was ignore me, and it was the most powerful thing anyone had ever done. It made me feel fucking helpless.

When I glanced back to Owen, he actually looked concerned for me. "That bad, huh?"

"I'm not used to anyone ignoring me," I said flatly.

"I don't think that's what's getting to you."

"All right, what's getting to me then?" I was irritable, and it was evident in my tone.

Owen shook his head slowly. "You don't know what the hell to do about Harlow. Since I'm the same way, it's easy to see. You like to plan things out, to manage them. There's a reason you're successful in business. Relationships aren't like business. There are factors beyond your control."

"Tell me something I don't know," I muttered, throwing a glare his way.

Chapter Thirty-One

HARLOW

The flames flashed high in the sky, bright in the darkness. I stood beside Susannah and watched as the roof fell in on the house. Although she and I weren't on the same crew, our crews had responded together to this fire. A ramshackle home on the outskirts of Willow Brook had caught fire. We wouldn't know until the fire was completely out, but all signs pointed to it starting in the woodstove. My best guess was that the owners hadn't bothered to clean the chimney before winter this year.

Time and again, that was what started fires. This fire had spread due to a few outbuildings being too close to the home. The owners were facing the destruction of all structures on the property. I only hoped they had good insurance. Everyone had gotten out safely, so we could worry about things, like insurance.

Glancing at Susannah, I took a deep breath and let it out with a sigh. "Well, everyone's safe and that's the best we can hope for in a situation like this."

Susannah nodded, resting a hand on her hip and tugging

her helmet off. "It is. When I heard that baby crying..." Her words trailed off.

The moment she spoke, a flash of anxiety pierced me. We had likely all experienced the same feeling when we heard the baby crying and realized the parents, along with their toddler and a months-old baby, were trapped upstairs with the fire completely engulfing the stairwell.

Ward approached us, stopping beside Susannah. "Now that the fire's under control, you two can head out. Some of us will stay until the fire cools down and it's safe to leave. Why don't you pick up Wayne from your parents on the way home?"

Susannah straightened, her eyes flicking to me as she shook her head, and then looked back to him. "I know you don't like it when he spends the night away from us, and I don't either, but I think it's better to just let him sleep. He's probably been asleep for hours now."

Ward didn't look thrilled with her reply, his eyes narrowing. He opened his mouth, about to say something, before he snapped it shut again, laughing softly. "I hate it when we're both on duty."

Susannah stepped closer, sliding her arm around his waist as he leaned over and dropped a kiss on her messy hair. "I hate it too, but it doesn't happen very often. Maybe once or twice a year both of our crews are on call for local stuff. I take it that means you're staying?"

Ward nodded. "Of course. You head home, and I'll see you in the morning."

Even though Susannah's face was streaked with soot, and she was wearing her heavy gear, the look Ward gave her was so intimate, I reflexively looked away.

After we returned to the station, Susannah and I were in the small locker room set aside for women. I was toweling off after my shower when Susannah spoke. "Are you okay?"

Glancing up, I met her concerned blue gaze. "Yeah, I'm..." I started to answer automatically.

My words trailed off because I wasn't fine. I missed Max, and I was ignoring him. Quite purposefully. Christmas was a week away, and no matter how many times I told myself it was just life, the holidays were treacherous for me. With the hand I had been dealt, I wasn't a huge fan of them. When you didn't have your own family to turn to, the loneliness was accentuated.

Susannah was a friend, and I knew she was only asking because she was worried. Aside from the holidays and that old lingering pain, I didn't know what the hell to do about Max. I hadn't realized I'd begun to expect him to text me daily until he stopped a few days ago. I worried that the very thing I told myself would be best had actually happened. He had decided to leave me alone.

"Actually, I'm not really fine. The holidays aren't my favorite time of year, and this thing with Max has got me all mixed up. I always want too much from men, so I decided it was best if I tried to keep some boundaries in place. And now I just miss him."

I didn't say aloud that it felt as if events kept conspiring to illuminate everything I wanted and everything I hoped for. Tonight's fire had been nothing out of the ordinary. Homes rarely reached the point of completely burning down, but dealing with it was simply part of my job.

The fire had been routine. I'd been the firefighter who'd gone up the ladder to help get the family out. By virtue of my smaller size, getting in and out of windows with my gear was often easier than for some of the guys. Everyone was safe, when all was said and done. What had scraped across my heart—my raw, far-too-vulnerable heart—had been witnessing the pure love I observed amongst the couple and their young children. As was usually the case, something like a fire brought everything into sharp focus for people. Boundaries went up in flames, and feelings that often bubbled under the surface were exposed.

For this young family, the only thing visible was love and

concern, the kind that ran deep as a river. The kind I wasn't so sure I would ever be lucky enough to have. Spinning that into the lingering loss from my miscarriage and missing Max, and I was a bit of an emotional wreck.

When I looked back to Susannah and saw the warmth and understanding in her eyes, I burst into tears. Tugging the towel around me, I sat down on the bench running in front of the lockers and buried my face in my hands. I felt Susannah sit down beside me, her arm sliding around my shoulders.

She didn't say anything for a few moments, allowing me the opportunity to gather myself. After a few minutes, I lifted my head and knuckled the tears away from my eyes.

"I'm kind of a mess," I muttered.

Susannah gave my shoulders a squeeze and slipped her arm away as she stood and walked to a counter running along the back wall. Snagging a box of tissues, she carried it over to me, sitting down on the bench across from me as I blew my nose.

"Okay, so it seems like Max might mean something to you. What do you want to do about it?" she asked matter-of-factly.

With the tissue balled in my hand, I stared at her. "That's the problem. I don't know."

Susannah was quiet, her gaze considering as she regarded me. "Have you two talked about this?"

My mind instantly flashed to all of the absolutely right things Max had said the night before he left, after which I began ignoring every overture from him. I finally nodded because I wasn't going to lie; that wouldn't be fair to Max. "We did. He says he wants me to give us a chance. I'm just worried that things are moving too fast and that he doesn't really know what he wants."

Susannah cocked her head to the side. "Unless you're really good at keeping things on the down low, you haven't dated anyone since you've been in Willow Brook. Is there a reason for that?"

I nodded, sniffling and knuckling at another tear rolling out of my eyes. "I don't have the best track record with men. I'm great at finding guys who aren't interested in anything serious, but tricking myself into thinking they might be. My last relationship was right before my miscarriage."

"Oh."

I sensed she wasn't sure quite what to say, or that she might say the wrong thing. We had talked about this before, but it was a loaded topic. "It's okay. I'm over that guy. He was a total dick. The hard part was the miscarriage."

"I'm just going to be blunt. I don't think you would be this upset if Max wasn't worth being upset over. If he wants you to give him a chance, then I think you should. Why not? What have you got to lose?"

"Um, my sanity."

Susannah laughed. "Fair enough, but you're already upset. Take it from me, it's worth it if it's the right thing. There's only one way to find out."

Obviously, she hadn't been privy to my conversations with Ivy, but she was hitting on the same point Ivy had made. In order for a relationship to have a chance, I had to *give* it a chance. I took a deep breath and stood from the bench to tug on my jeans. We finished getting dressed. Susannah was quiet, allowing me the time to mull things over.

"I suppose I just need to figure out how to go about this," I eventually said, as I closed my locker.

She turned to face me, rubbing her towel over her damp hair once more and tossing it in the hamper in the corner. "I'm a fan of direct. It just makes it easier."

I laughed. "I suppose it does."

I was tugging on my jacket when she asked me another question. "Ward mentioned some guy applied for one of the crews for next summer. He told Ward he used to work with you. Do you happen to know him?"

Oh, this was awkward. Speaking of direct, I figured that was my best option here. "I do. He's the guy that I dated for a little while. I got pregnant while I was on the pill. You know the rest. You might not know that he was screwing around with two other women there. I've been thinking I should mention to Ward what went down, but it seems weird."

Susannah's eyes narrowed as she rested a hand on her hip. "Hell no. That's not weird shit. I mean, sure, it's personal. But it's all about trust, which is critical for any hotshot crew. If a guy's gonna pull bullshit like that, we don't need him here. If you don't want to tell Ward, I will."

Her response surprised me, and it must've shown on my face. She continued, "Seriously, that's bullshit. Your call. Either you tell Ward, or I will."

"I'll do it. Obviously, I won't do it tonight, but I'll find him tomorrow."

We walked out of the station together into the cold darkness. Pausing at the back of my truck, Susannah looked to me. "Don't miss out."

Chapter Thirty-Two

MAX

I decided to embrace the concept of flying blind. I didn't know what the hell was the best approach with Harlow, but I was done waiting. Owen had agreed to stay a few extra days in Anchorage, and I was driving to Willow Brook.

The sky was bright blue, and the roads were blessedly clear. I'd have driven through a snowstorm to get to her, but I didn't mind the weather being on my side. Not much later, I rolled into Willow Brook. I didn't even stop in town, I headed straight for her house. When I got there to find her truck gone, I turned right back around.

When I reached the station, I was relieved to see her truck out back. I didn't want to take liberties, so I parked in front. Needless to say, I was startled to find her father sitting in the waiting area.

Howard May was a tall, imposing man. He had silver hair and stark features. He was seated in a chair, looking quite impatient, and didn't see me at first. He glanced up, looking toward Maisie, who was at the reception counter taking a call. "If you don't mind, I've been waiting ten minutes," he said sharply.

"For God's sake, Howard, she's a dispatcher. Maybe you think you're important, but somebody else's life might actually be on the line," I said, unable to hold myself back from commenting.

Howard's gaze swung to me, his dark eyes narrowing as he stood. "What the hell are you doing here, Max?"

For a beat, I considered not saying a word about my involvement with his daughter. Before I had a chance to answer, the door to the back opened and Harlow emerged. From the look on her face alone, I could guess that Maisie had let her know her father was here. Her features were drawn, and there were two bright pink spots on her cheeks. Her shoulders were tense as her eyes bounced from her father to me, widening when she saw me.

Speaking of flying blind, I didn't know what the hell to do now. Obviously, I didn't plan to show up here at the same time as her father.

Howard turned to her and barked, "Well, it's about damn time. I've been waiting almost fifteen minutes."

"Dad, I was in the middle of something. I know you don't consider this job important, but I do," she said sharply. "What are you doing here?"

"You haven't been returning my calls. It's almost Christmas, and I wanted to know what your plans were. Your mother's parents left a message with me. They would love to see you."

Harlow looked as if she was floundering, a mix of emotions passing across her face.

Howard turned back to me when she didn't reply. "And you didn't answer, what the hell are you doing here?"

Harlow surprised me, stepping to my side. "He's here to see me, Dad."

Howard looked between us, a sense of confusion crossing his face. Just when I was wondering how much she intended to say to her father about us, I felt her hand curl around mine. "I met Max last year at Owen and Ivy's wedding. We're seeing each other."

My heart started to thud, banging against my ribs. Emotion crashed over me, and I wished like hell Howard wasn't our audience right now. All I could do was follow Harlow's lead at this point, so I squeezed her hand, gratified when she squeezed back.

"I'm spending Christmas with Ivy and Owen..."

For a moment, I tuned out. *That's where I'll be for Christmas then. Don't forget to call Mom to let her know later.*

Harlow's voice drew me back from my mental interruption. "I'll call Grandmother and let her know. She has my number, so I'm not sure why she didn't call me directly. I have to say, I'm not sure why you're here, Dad. I thought you were done with me."

I could feel the subtle tremor of tension running through her and knew this was hard on her. I had seen Howard in action in negotiations before. He had succeeded in business, in part, because he was ruthless and cold. I could only imagine what it had been like to be a child around him. Not that this was a negotiation, but Howard approached everything like that.

Harlow's father stared at her and then rolled his eyes, sliding a hand in his pocket. Obviously, the man had flown all the way to Alaska and hunted down his daughter here in this small town on the edge of the wilderness. He clearly wanted to see her for some reason. Yet, for the life of me, I didn't know what he wanted from her.

"I might have acted hastily in saying that I was done with you," he finally said. For the first time ever, I saw a hint of vulnerability in Howard. "If you reconsider..."

Harlow cut him off. "Dad, I won't reconsider working for you. I don't know what's going to happen, but it won't be that."

Howard's mouth tightened, and he looked away before nodding slowly. I caught Maisie's eyes across the room. She looked worried. I was relieved, not only for my presence here, but for Maisie's. Harlow was used to being alone. The simple fact that she wasn't alone in facing her father felt important to me, no matter how brief the interaction.

Howard finally looked back at her and then to me. "Max is a good man."

"I know he is, Dad," Harlow said, her tone startled. "Don't take this the wrong way, but your opinion of any man in my life isn't a mark in their favor. I know Max is a good man because of how he's treated me. I'm not sure why you're here, and if you'd like to stay in touch again, just let me know. But right now, I need to talk to Max."

Howard stared at her before slowly inclining his head again. I wondered if he had ever even hugged his daughter. He didn't now. Instead, he stepped closer and lifted a hand, awkwardly squeezing her shoulder. "Okay then. I'll be traveling over the holidays, but you know how to reach me if you need anything."

Stepping back, Howard looked between Harlow and me, his gaze considering. Though I didn't know Howard outside of the business, I sensed he actually might have been a little hurt with Harlow's clear boundary. Despite his absent approach to parenting, his daughter was one of the most amazing people I knew. Whether she got all of those characteristics from her mother or not, at least I could say Howard hadn't taken that away from her.

Knowing how he approached business, I imagined his relationship with Harlow as an adult would be much the same. His savvy negotiation tactics and ruthlessness certainly weren't going to win Harlow over.

For a moment, I experienced a stab of empathy for him. After a moment of tense silence, his gaze locked on me. "You treat her right, or you'll have to answer to me."

Harlow saved me from answering. She rolled her eyes, her breath coming out in a huff. "Seriously? You've never had an opinion on my love life. I don't think you've ever even asked about it," she said, her tone almost disbelieving.

Howard cut his eyes to her. "Well, you've never talked to me about it. I know I haven't been the best father, but I do care about you. Call me if you need anything."

At that not-so-warm statement, Howard started to turn away.

"Howard," I called. He spun back, lifting a brow. "You have my word I'll treat her right."

Once again, his gaze bounced between us. With a subtle nod, he turned and left, walking out into the winter afternoon.

This entire time, Maisie had been sitting quietly, as our audience at the reception desk where she took dispatch calls. Harlow looked to me and then to Maisie, her expression confused. Just as I squeezed Harlow's hand, Maisie spoke.

"Well, I don't know your dad too well, and he doesn't exactly seem like the warm and fuzzy kind, but I guess that went okay?"

Harlow held my hand tight in hers as she turned and took a few steps to rest her elbow on the counter circling Maisie. I'd braced myself for all kinds of eventualities this afternoon, but this last encounter with her father had blindsided me. At this point, I was simply following Harlow's lead on everything.

"No, he's not warm and fuzzy," she said with a little laugh.

"Are you okay?" Maisie asked.

Harlow cocked her head to the side, her eyes bouncing to mine briefly. "I suppose so. As weird as the conversation might've been, it's probably the nicest my dad has ever been." A little laugh escaped, and she shook her head slowly. "That was just weird."

When she looked to me, as if for some kind of confirmation, I shrugged. "That was certainly like no other conversation I've had with your father."

At that, she threw her head back with a full-throated laugh, the sound sending a hot jolt through me. Jesus. *This* woman. She had the craziest effect on me. Nothing about this particular moment was conducive to lust, but then, nothing about Harlow was conducive to anything sensible or rational.

The sound of her throaty laugh and the feel of her hand in mine sent a score of lust through me. Everything was tangled up together when it came to Harlow. Conveniently, the dispatch line buzzed, and Maisie waved us away as she took the call, her tone shifting to all business.

Harlow nodded her head toward the door that led into the back of the station. Seeing as trying to have a conversation of the likes I wanted wouldn't exactly take place in the waiting area, I followed.

Hell, I'd have followed Harlow anywhere right now.

Chapter Thirty-Three

HARLOW

With Max's hand warm around mine, the calloused pad of his thumb brushing across my knuckles, I led him into the back of the station. My heart was beating hard and fast, while my stomach felt as if I had just taken a dive out of a plane.

Today had been one revelation after another. I had woken up to a text from Cliff, of all people. Like I said, I was well over him. I hadn't been thrilled to hear he might be coming up here and had been a bit relieved at Susannah's vehement and protective reaction to learning he was planning to apply here for a summer position.

Not that I had rewritten our history in my mind, but he had promptly reinforced all of it with a single text.

Hi, hoping you don't mind putting in a good word for me. I'd like to take on one of the temporary summer positions up there. The money is good. If I like it, maybe I'll stay.

That was it. That was all my ex had to say. He hadn't even bothered to ask how I was doing. But then, that was how bad my judgment had been with him. My tendency to be polite had my thumbs hovering over the screen to reply.

Then, I remembered that I didn't owe Cliff anything. Instead of replying, I had ignored it and blocked his number.

I didn't miss him at all, and I was clear-eyed about what he'd actually meant to me—in genuine terms, not in wishful terms. All I had to do was think about Max to put that relationship—or rather, non-relationship—in perspective.

I'd come into the station and gone straight to Ward to let him know precisely why I didn't recommend he hire Cliff. I left out all the details, except for the fact that he slept around amongst the crews and lied about it. Ward had been nothing but gracious, and I sensed Susannah might have given him a little bit more information. He was tactful enough not to bring it up.

Only minutes after that, Maisie had buzzed me to let me know my father was here. Before that, I had promised myself I was going to scramble up the courage to call Max because if anything could have cast my feelings for him into sharp relief, Cliff's text most certainly had.

When I'd walked out to meet my father and found Max waiting, an immense sense of relief had washed through me. Without a word passing between us, I knew he had my back when it came to my father. I would have plenty of time to contemplate what had prompted my father to show up like that, but right now, my priority was Max.

Beck happened to be walking out of his office. *Perfect.* I called, "Beck?"

He was heading down the hallway toward the kitchen, and spun back. "Yeah?"

"I don't suppose I could borrow your office for a few minutes."

Beck looked curiously from me to Max before nodding. "Of course. I actually need to run to the hardware store. Let me just grab my jacket."

Stepping back into the office, he snagged his jacket off the back of his desk chair, gesturing us through the door. "It's all yours. I'll be back in a bit."

When the door shut behind him, my anxiety notched up to an eleven on a scale of one to ten. The abstract concept of letting Max know I was willing to give us a shot was a lot easier than actually doing it. We were alone now.

He still held my hand where we stood by the door, his familiar gaze canting down to meet mine. With butterflies taking flight in my belly, I looked up at him. It had been too many days and I had missed seeing him. I absorbed the sight of him—his icy blue eyes, and the clean, strong lines of his face. He had more than a five o'clock shadow at this point, and I loved it.

"Well, that was a surprise," he said.

"Seeing my dad, you mean?"

"No. You."

"Me, what?"

"You not ignoring me," he clarified, his mouth hitching up at the corner and sending a delicious streak of heat through me.

"I was going to call you today, but you're here."

"I am. What were you going to call me about?"

He turned to face me more fully, the gravelly sound of his voice sending a shiver chasing over my skin.

This man. All he had to do was be near me and turn the intensity of his focus to me, and I melted. My heart and body surrendered to him. My emotions were so close to the surface, pressing against my skin to get out. I tried to take a deep breath, but air was hard to come by. My pulse was racing, and I felt hot all over; almost feverish, ablaze with a mix of desire and emotion.

"I was going to tell you that you were right," I finally said, my voice coming out breathy.

"Right about what?"

Oh geez, he was going to make me spell it out.

"That we should give us a chance." Giving voice to my deepest desires was hard, much harder than I had imagined. When they weren't abstract, the gravity was overwhelming.

Max's gaze held mine for a few beats, the look in his eyes so intense, it seared me to my soul.

"Oh, thank God," he muttered fiercely.

In a hot second, he fit his mouth over mine. Our kiss was rough and fierce, pent-up emotion pouring into every stroke, every nip, and every mingled breath. I had been holding back inside. Letting go was akin to water rushing down a mountain in spring, the ice melting and breaking loose.

Sometimes words just wouldn't do.

His tongue swept into my mouth, a guttural groan coming from his throat. One of his hands tangled in my hair, while the other swept down my spine to cup my bottom, palming my ass and rocking his hips into me. His arousal was hot and hard, resting at the apex of my thighs.

He drew back, his teeth catching my bottom lip before he released it gently. His forehead fell to mine.

"You make me crazy, Harlow," he murmured against my lips.

I was caught in a wave of emotion. Tears pressed hot at the backs of my eyes.

Drawing back, his eyes narrowed in concern. "What's wrong?"

"Nothing," I said swiftly, shaking my head and swiping at my tears just as he brushed his thumb across my cheek to catch one. "It's just a lot. Not bad, all good."

The tension in his face eased slightly. "I have no idea what I'm doing, just so you know. All I know is I had to come here today. I couldn't take it, not knowing what was going on with you. I was trying to give you space, but it turns out I'm not so good at that."

A laugh slipped out. Seeing Max Channing, a wealthy man who had the world at his fingertips when he chose, looking a little lost and uncertain was simultaneously humbling, overwhelming, and amusing.

His mouth curled into a grin, and he shrugged. "I don't mind admitting you bring me to my knees." His gaze sobered as he brushed my hair back from my face, sliding his fingers through it and tucking a loose lock behind my ear. A little shiver ran down that side, a trail of goose bumps chasing in the wake of his touch.

"I was worried that I said too much too soon," he murmured.

Emotion was tight in my throat, but I breathed through it and held his gaze. "You didn't say too much too soon. I needed to hear it to kick my butt in gear." I paused, trying to gather myself. I was unsteady inside, with emotion and need spinning wildly. I was also plain overwhelmed at having Max right here in front of me.

Max all by himself, was intense. His physical presence was overwhelming. All it took was a look, and he stole my breath and sent my senses spinning.

Although I meant what I said—I *had* planned to call him today and tell him I wanted to give us a chance—I hadn't thought through what to say. Just now, with the heat of him close, one hand resting on my bottom and the other on the curve of my neck, his thumb brushing idly over the wild thrum of my pulse, I couldn't think clearly. At all. My heart was practically stomping its feet, throwing a little tantrum in order to be heard over the cacophony of my thoughts that usually snuffed it out.

"I didn't expect to fall in love with you."

Well, *that* just slipped right out without my permission. Saying the word *love* aloud sent a bolt of sheer terror through me. I was so accustomed to trying to love people who weren't present to return it, and reading love into every small gesture when it wasn't even there.

Max's eyes blazed bright. "You don't have to say that until you're sure."

I recalled his words, days ago now, when he said he hadn't planned on falling in love with me, and my argument that it was too soon. In truth, it had been over a year ago now when our lives had first collided in a single, utterly unforgettable night. My body and heart had known the potential contained between us then.

There was no room for doubt. I shook my head. "I know I don't have to say anything, but I meant it. I don't think I'm falling in love with you, I *am* in love with you."

I had all kinds of reasons why the idea of love in reality scared me. Max didn't leave me room to say any more, tracing my lips with his thumb before he fit his mouth over mine, spiraling us right back to where we'd been— in another hot, wild kiss. Then he was spinning us around, bringing my back flush to the door, as I curled my legs around his hips and tried to imprint myself against him. He held me easily in his arms, his lips blazing a trail of fire down my neck.

There was a sudden knock at the door. I abruptly remembered we were in Beck's office at the station. Max drew away, not letting me go just yet.

"Beck," Cade's voice called.

"Oh my God," I hissed. "You have to let me down."

Max grinned, easing me down slowly. I took a deep breath, attempting to gather myself and open the door, but then I heard Maisie's voice. "He ran to the hardware store," she called down the hallway to Cade.

"Well, you could've told me," he replied, as his footsteps retreated away from the door.

Turning back, I caught Max's sly grin.

"I think we should probably go," I murmured, hoping my blush was fading.

"Please tell me you're not working for the rest of the day," he said bluntly, his hot gaze sweeping up and down, lingering over my breasts. My nipples practically stood up and waved at him.

I shook my head. "No, I was just finishing up for the day as it was."

"Let's go."

In a matter of minutes, we were in his new vehicle. It was

an all-black SUV—hybrid, of course, and decked out with every imaginable bit of tech. It reminded me of Owen's vehicle, the very vehicle where I'd met Max when he picked me up at the hotel to take me to Ivy's wedding.

I never thought I'd think fondly and romantically about a vehicle, but in this moment, I did. Glancing over, I asked, "Did you just buy this here?"

He flicked his gaze to the side as he turned onto Main Street, heading out of downtown toward my house. "Technically yes, but I arranged delivery of it after Owen and I finalized the deal for the company. I knew I'd be up here a bit, so I needed my own vehicle. It just came in a few days ago."

Only then did I realize I hadn't even bothered to follow him in my truck, so it was back at the station. It was a damn miracle I remembered to get my jacket and purse.

"I forgot my truck."

Max's low chuckle sent a little thrill through me. "You don't need it."

The door slammed shut behind us. Max caught my hand in his and reeled me to him, spinning me around. My back bounced against the door as his mouth collided with mine, picking up right where we'd left off in Beck's office.

With his mouth hot over mine, I climbed him like a tree. Curling my legs around his hips, I looped my arms around his neck and tumbled into the madness. A rushing sensation poured through me; everything I'd been trying to tamp down and hold back had been let loose, and I was caught in the tide. With his hard, strong body against mine, and his lips breaking free to tease along my jaw, his tongue swirling in the shell of my ear and sending a hot shiver over my skin, all I knew was I needed more. *Now.* My head thumped against the door, and I murmured, "You have too many clothes on."

Max had been busy working at the buttons of my blouse with his lips teasing along my collarbone. The feel of his low laugh against my skin made me giggle.

"I could say the same of you," he replied as he lifted his head, his eyes dark. "Let's take care of that."

As he started to step back, I faced a problem. I didn't want to let him go. Yet, in order for him to remove those cumbersome clothes, I had no choice. He tried to move away, and I tightened my hold on him. "I don't want to let you go."

Suddenly, what had started out as a tease got caught in the riptide of emotion tugging at me. A sense of vulnerability slammed into me.

Max's palm came up to cradle my cheek, his thumb brushing over my lips. "What is it?"

I shook my head, swallowing through the emotion knotting in my chest and throat. "It's just a lot," I finally managed to say, my voice thick.

"I know."

There were so many things I needed to say, but it was all too much. For the moment, I needed to lose myself in the storm of sensation whipping around us. Reading me easily, Max held me close as he turned away from the door.

"One thing at a time," he murmured, his lips dusting across my temple as he spoke. "Right now, I need to be inside of you."

"Okay, that would be perfect," I said, almost breathless.

He eased me down. Our clothes came off in a messy rush. His hands mapped me, his lips, teeth, and tongue teasing my skin as I collapsed onto the couch. It was all perfect. The scrape of his stubble on my breast, and his teeth closing over a nipple. The exquisite feel of his weight bearing down over me, then the intense pleasure of his fingers sliding into my channel, curving and hitting that sweet spot, sending desire sizzling through me.

Everything was a blur of sensation. One thing held true all this time. Even the very first time Max's lips met mine, there had been nothing to hide, nothing to hold back.

Still shuddering, pleasure spun in my core, radiating outward. I dragged my eyes open as Max rose above me, settling his hips between my thighs. We hadn't even bothered to try to make it to a bed. That was how desperate we were to be bare and tangled up in each other.

He slid home inside of me in one swift surge, his blue gaze searing me with its intensity. Skin to skin, heartbeat to heartbeat, he filled me completely, the stretch of him sending pleasure scoring through me as he began to move.

The intimacy that had frightened me before was still slightly terrifying right now. Yet, in the warmth of his gaze, I held on tight and we rode through the storm together. It was raw pleasure, with nothing but the feel of his hard body and the strength of him surrounding me. Every stroke pushed me higher and higher as another climax began to build from the echoes of the last.

Reaching between us as pleasure began to scatter through me, he pressed his thumb over my clit and sent me flying again. With my name a rough chant, his release poured into me as I shuddered from my own climax.

The moment he fell against me, he moved to shift his weight off me, but I curled my legs around his hips tightly. "No, I like your weight."

He rose up on his elbow slightly, looking down at me. "I don't like crushing you. Here, we'll compromise," he murmured, as he shifted slightly so we were resting at an angle on the couch.

We lay still and quiet for a few moments. My fingers circled lightly on his chest, and he loosened a hand tangled in my hair.

"So, you're going to Diamond Creek for Christmas?"

Shifting slightly, I leaned back so I could see his face. "Yes, that's the plan. What about you?"

When I wasn't caught in the fire of need blazing between us and reality hit me, I started to get anxious. Just now, with his eyes searching mine, unease tightened in my chest.

"Oh, I'll be in Diamond Creek. Unless you tell me not to go. I might argue the point with you, though," he said with a low chuckle.

His sly grin and the gleam in his eyes tugged a laugh from me, easing the anxiety spinning inside. "I'm not planning to tell you not to go. Why would you think that?"

His shoulder rose and fell in an easy shrug. "I had no idea what to expect today. I came to make my case. Thank God you let me off easy. But I know you might want to take things slower than I prefer."

As I stared into his eyes, my heart flew skyward, akin to a bird escaping from its cage. The sense of freedom was immense. "I hadn't really thought things through, but let's start with Christmas."

He dipped his head, pressing his lips to mine. "I suppose we should have the next part of this conversation before you start worrying."

"What makes you think I'll start worrying?"

I was partly teasing, but it was slightly unsettling how quickly he'd come to understand the way my mind worked. The downside to my haphazard childhood, and the loss of the primary source of stability in it—my mother—was that I was always looking ahead, wondering and worrying about what might happen next.

I had created a life for myself where I could manage those contingencies. I wasn't sure how to fit a man into that, much less the man I happened to fall in love with.

Even though the depth of my feelings slightly terrified me, and probably would for a while now, I didn't question my feelings for Max. You'd have to beat me away from him with a stick at this point. Yet, I knew the practicalities of our lives didn't quite mesh easily.

He promptly demonstrated his mind-reading abilities. "If we're going to do this, there are a few practical issues to discuss. Rather than worrying about it, how about we agree that until you decide if you want to leave here, I'll work from Anchorage? I'll commute. We'll figure it out."

My mouth must've fallen open because he smiled ruefully. "I can tell you like it here. I'm not gonna take that away from you. It might surprise you, but I'm not particularly attached to living in the city. I'll have to travel some, there's no doubt about that, but I can make it work. Hell, Owen runs a similar setup in Diamond Creek. I just wanted to make it crystal clear that I'll do whatever it takes."

The emotion I thought I had gotten a handle on spun wildly inside. I hadn't thought this part through, mostly because I'd only come to terms with facing my feelings for Max over the last few days. I certainly hadn't expected him to make this part so easy for me.

Tears pricked in my eyes again, and I didn't realize one was rolling down my cheek until I felt his thumb brush it away. "I didn't mean to make you cry."

A giggle slipped out. "I think that was a happy tear, just one. I do like it here, but we'll find a way to make it work. If that means moving to San Francisco, I'll do that too. It happens to be a city I love."

"Now you're making it complicated," Max replied, his mouth curling in a grin.

EPILOGUE

Max

Christmas, one year later

I looked across the room, watching as Harlow stepped through the archway into the restaurant at Last Frontier Lodge. Her glossy dark hair was loose, and she wore the same dress she'd been wearing the first time I saw her—a slip of cream silk that caressed her curves. It wasn't quite suited for this weather, but she pointed out she didn't have to go outside.

A full year had passed since our first Christmas together, and Harlow had insisted we celebrate Christmas here again this year. Seeing as I said yes to anything she asked of me, I was happy to go along. The holiday lights glittered around the restaurant. Through the windows circling the lodge, one of the many surrounding spruce trees was decorated with lights, twinkling in the darkness and illuminating the snow drifting down.

My eyes tracked Harlow as she approached, savoring the swing of her hips, and the graceful motion as she brushed her hair back over her shoulder. When she reached me where I was sitting on a stool at the bar, I didn't bother being polite. I slipped my arm around her waist, letting it slide over the silk to cup her bottom as I pulled her in between my knees.

She giggled, her breath coming out in a little puff. "Max, you know we're in public, right?"

"Of course I do. I still don't give a damn," I murmured, just as I brought my lips to her plump lips. Despite her minor protest, she kissed me, her tongue sliding against mine.

I heeded her warning because I had enough sense to know that when Harlow kissed me, I lost sight of everything but her. I could only let myself have a tease, or we'd be in trouble. When I drew away, her cheeks were pink and her eyes dark.

Garrett's amused voice punctured our moment. "Need a drink, Harlow?" I glanced over, catching his wink. "Sorry to break things up."

"I'll take a pomegranate martini," Harlow said.

"That's the drink you had at the wedding."

"You remember that?" she asked, her eyes widening.

"Of course I do. When it comes to you, I remember every detail." I held her close, savoring the heat of her skin through the silk.

Garrett handed over her drink, and she eventually stepped away, sliding onto the stool beside me when Ivy and Owen came over to join us. We had promised my parents we would be visiting for New Year's, but I was fairly certain we would probably spend every Christmas here.

It was one of Harlow's favorite places, and because it reminded me of her, it happened to be one of mine as well. It didn't hurt to have our respective best friends here.

"Yo," Owen's voice said from my side.

I'd zoned out, savoring the feel of Harlow's hand in mind. "Yeah?" I asked, glancing to him.

"Was it worth it?" he asked.

I knew he was referring to our conversation just over a year ago, when he told me if I thought Harlow was worth it, I'd better do something about it.

"Every fucking minute. Best thing I ever did was marry her as soon as she said yes."

That particular moment happened to have been entirely unplanned. As was always the case when it came to Harlow, my propensity for methodical planning fell by the wayside. We had gone out for coffee one morning early last spring. We were staying in Willow Brook, and I'd been about to leave that morning to take a plane down to San Francisco. Though I had gotten her engagement ring weeks prior, intending to ask her to marry me at exactly the right time, that time turned out to be over coffee at Firehouse Café.

Conveniently, I learned that same morning that Janet James was ordained to marry people. As soon as Harlow said yes, I persuaded Janet to do the honors.

Owen chuckled, his eyes shifting to Ivy, who sat beside him, and then back to Harlow on the other side of me. "Told you. It's not hard when it's the right thing."

"Hell no, easiest decision I ever made."

A lot had happened in the past year. For starters, I'd discovered Harlow could be quite indecisive. She hemmed and hawed about what to do and where we should live. I was so accustomed to travel and a brutal schedule that staying with her in Willow Brook and commuting to Anchorage wasn't a hardship.

I even scheduled my other travel around when she had to go out in the backcountry for fires. I didn't love that, but it was part of who Harlow was, so I accepted it.

A few weeks ago, she announced she wanted to try to get pregnant soon. I'd been prepared to make my case that I would've been concerned about her keeping her job. Bless-edly, she saved me the battle.

Now we just had to figure out what we wanted to do

next. As far as her getting pregnant, I was nothing if not a planner. Not that we needed anything to motivate us, but it was fair to say I might've been wearing her out, even though she was still on birth control. I figured practice makes perfect.

Just now, I caught her hand in mine and pulled her close. Dipping my head as she leaned forward, I pressed a kiss along that sweet spot on the side of her neck, savoring the hint of vanilla and honey she always carried. "How much longer do we have to stay to be polite?" I murmured.

————

HARLOW

I felt my cheeks heat, and a shiver run through me at Max's words. I had wondered if the effect he had on me would wear off; if anything, the opposite seemed to be true. The longer we were together, the more I wanted him.

I drew away, catching the slight gleam in his eye. "I just got here a few minutes ago."

He shrugged unabashedly. "I'll wait."

He slipped his arm around my waist, tugging the stool I was sitting on closer to his. We passed the time, laughing and chatting with friends as Christmas lights glittered around us. For two Christmases in a row, I'd been surrounded by people who loved me and who I loved in return.

I doubted Max could ever know what a gift that was. My father and I still had a slightly distant relationship, but the fact that we spoke at all was a win, given his feelings about me refusing to work for him.

I didn't make Max wait too long, if only because I didn't want to wait either. Later that night, after he'd once again left me satiated, I stood by the windows in the lodge, looking out into the night sky. The snow had lightened with only a few flakes drifting down, sparkling in the holiday lights surrounding the lodge.

A shimmer of the Northern Lights glimmered faintly in the distance. "Look," I said softly, pointing to the subtle shades of pink and purple.

Max came up behind me, sliding his hands around my waist, and dipped his head to drop a kiss on my neck. "At you?" he asked.

"Oh my God, you're ridiculous. The Northern Lights," I murmured, gasping when his stubble scraped my neck.

"Ah, I didn't notice. You're too distracting."

And just like that, my heart melted.

————

Thank you for reading Melt With You - I hope you loved Max & Harlow's story!

Up next in the Into the Fire Series is Burn For You - Holly & Nate's story. Friends to lovers, second chance & more! Holly's all about giving to a good cause. Until Nate wins a date with her at a charity date auction. F*ck. Nate drives Holly crazy, in all the wrong ways. Oh, and he's her brothers' best friend. Talk about complicated.

Keep reading for a sneak peek!

Be sure to sign up for my newsletter for the latest news, teasers & more! Click here to sign up: http://jhcroixauthor.com/subscribe/

EXCERPT: BURN FOR YOU

Holly

PSA: Dating sucks.

I was staring down thirty—two years away was too close, as far as I was concerned—and not really looking forward to it. I was additionally annoyed with myself for actually caring about the fact that I was turning thirty. I didn't like to think of myself as one of those women who obsessed over her age.

Apparently, I was. Or at least, lately. You see, all my friends kept falling in love. I was happy for them. I truly was. Cross my heart and hope to die, I was not exaggerating about that. But, well, I was starting to feel left behind. My friends were even having babies. Babies! And I'd yet to even find a man, or woman, or mythical creature, much less procreate. I refused to let myself become one of those bitter spinsters.

That said, trying to date in a small town in Alaska had its challenges. I loved Willow Brook. It was my hometown, and I'd never been the kind of person who needed to leave to remember how much I loved it. Not that there was anything wrong with that. I had tons of friends and family, and I couldn't imagine living anywhere else. But *you* try meeting someone new when most everybody in town has known you since you were in preschool.

Correction: since you were a baby. But I didn't remember the baby stuff, so I sure as hell hoped nobody else did either. All of this led to a point. Or rather, a place and an event, and the reason why I was there.

I adjusted my rather tight nurse costume. In real life, nurses like myself wore scrubs and practical shoes. *Not* so sexy. In fact, comfort and getting bloodstains out was more important than looking good. The whole nurse costume thing was considered sexy, which had always cracked me up. Trust me, when you dealt with bodily fluids and seeing people often at their most vulnerable, there was very little about it that was sexy.

I loved my job, though. I was one of the head Emergency Department nurses at Willow Brook Hospital. I was living in my favorite place, doing work I loved. Even helping random tourists get fishing hooks out of God knows where on their body felt worthy.

Great job, great town, great friends and family ... and a whopping *zero* dating prospects for me. That was what probably landed me in my current situation. Somehow, I'd gotten roped into offering myself up for a date for a hospital fundraiser in Anchorage. The only reason I agreed was because I thought it'd be funny as hell. No one here would know me, and maybe, just maybe, I'd actually meet someone.

With Anchorage close to an hour away from Willow Brook, the possibility of meeting someone new shimmered on the invisible horizon. Plus, Anchorage was an actual city.

Standing backstage, I was a little nervous. Not only was this an auctioned date function, but it was for Halloween. Hence, why I was wearing a costume. For the first time since I'd become a nurse, I was dressed sexy.

Damn, even I had to admit I looked good. My rather annoyingly generous breasts were squished into this nurse costume, practically spilling out the top.

I'm sure you can imagine it. One of those tight little white numbers, with buttons up the middle of the fitted blouse, like no nurse would ever wear. It was snug at my waist and then flared out into a short little skirt, which barely covered my too-big ass. I was feeling slightly self-conscious.

My old friend from nursing school, Megan, had not informed me just how suggestive these costumes would be. I felt like a stripper.

"Oh my God, you look great," Megan said, as if she'd managed to read my mind from the other room. She closed the door behind her as she stepped into the small dressing room behind the stage.

The fundraiser was being held in a large auditorium in downtown Anchorage, frequently used for local performances and the like.

"You neglected to mention how small this was," I said, pinning her with a glare.

Megan shrugged. "You look totally hot. I'm doing it too. See?" she said, gesturing up and down her body.

"How come you got the fisher-girl outfit?" I asked as I scanned her costume.

She was wearing bright red fishing waders and a silky fitted tank top. Don't get me wrong, it was revealing, but it wasn't nearly as revealing as what I was wearing.

Megan grinned. "You're way sexier than me. I've got no ass to speak of, and you've got curves for days. I'm not back here to debate your costume, though. You're up in about ten minutes. I'm so glad you agreed to do this! I think you're gonna make the most money for us tonight."

"You sound like my pimp. I'm honored."

Megan was unmoved. She simply winked. "I'm happy to be your pimp. If you want me to find your man, I'm all over that shit. Come on," she said, gesturing for me to follow her. "I wish we'd saved you for last because you're definitely the hottest."

Seeing as most of my best friends were married, engaged, pregnant, or on the way to being pregnant, Megan was one of the few friends I confided in lately about my man troubles. Like me, she was still single. Unlike me, she wasn't really looking.

As I walked through the hallway, which was crowded with people prepping for the fundraiser, my belly started to coil with anxiety, and I felt flushed with heat. I suddenly realized this was an absolutely insane thing to do. The idea of it had seemed amusing and cute from a distance. But now, with my boobs nearly bursting out of my nurse costume, my butt just barely covered, and my bright red high heels, I was feeling just a teensy bit self-conscious.

Conveniently, there was alcohol backstage. I stopped by the bar, which was nothing more than a plastic table set up in the back, and smiled at the man behind it. He flashed a grin.

"What can I get you, dear? You look gorgeous, and you're going to make us a ton of money."

Inhaling a gulp of air, I let it out with a sigh. This man wasn't looking at me like he was going to eat me up, so I felt okay. "I'll take two shots of tequila," I replied.

The man's smile softened. "I would reconsider and stick with one. I'm Ethan, by the way."

"I'm Holly," I returned. "I still think I need two shots. How did you get roped into being a backstage bartender?"

Ethan chuckled as he poured me a single shot—generous, but just one. "My partner Jack and I own the Midnight Sun Arts galleries here in Anchorage and a few other locations. We help run a number of fundraisers. This is a good one. Absolutely all of the money raised goes into a funding pool to cover uninsured patients at hospitals all over Alaska. That's why we do so much on this one. Everybody you see here is volunteering."

He handed me my first shot. "Let's start with one."

"Oh no," I said with a shake of my head. "I've got ten minutes. I need two."

I gulped down the first shot, the burn of it quick and satisfying. Ethan eyed me and poured another shot. After my second one, I felt like I might have enough liquid courage to get me through this madness.

Ethan chatted with me while I waited, his easygoing manner calming me. Within a few minutes, Megan was ushering me out onto the stage.

As soon as I stepped out, I relaxed. It helped that I was just tipsy enough not to give much of a damn. I did my thing as instructed, walking across the stage and spinning in a circle, almost losing my balance in the process. Thank God I couldn't really see the crowd with the bright lights, seeing as my wobble got a laugh.

The auctioneer handled the bidding. Before I knew it, someone had "bought" a date with me for five thousand dollars. You heard me right—five thousand dollars.

Dizzy and more than a little buzzed by the time I got off the stage, I walked backstage. Megan flashed me a wink and a giant thumbs-up. Ethan, who I decided was my new best friend, shepherded me to a room where I was allegedly going to meet whoever the hell purchased a charity date with me. He paused outside the door, offering a warm smile.

"Well, dear, this man definitely wanted you. You just beat the last highest bid we've ever had by two grand."

All I could manage was a nod. With the tequila hitting me harder, I didn't care anymore. Crazy as this had been, at least I raised five thousand dollars for the hospital program. Ethan ushered me into a small room in the back where there was a table with a few bottles of alcohol and two chairs. They seemed to think if they scattered alcohol everywhere, people would be stupid enough to do this. I supposed I was the example of why they were right. I didn't really know how this thing worked. Apparently, my date could either have the date with me tonight, or later. I was thinking tonight was not the best plan, considering my tipsy state.

Within a minute, the door opened again. The moment my eyes landed on the man in question, my mouth fell open. Instead of my date, Nate Fox stepped into the room—all six-feet-four-inches of him with shaggy brown curls, flashing brown eyes, and a body made for sin.

Nate Fox was also my twin brother's best friend and the younger brother of my best friend's husband.

Even worse, I totally had a thing for Nate. In fact, one drunken night, about a year ago, we'd come dangerously close to fucking each other in the coat closet at a friend's party.

My twin brother had conveniently interrupted us. Alex was so oblivious, he didn't even pick up on the cues. Or perhaps he did and preferred to ignore my hastily yanked together blouse, which I later discovered had been buttoned lopsided.

Despite crossing paths almost weekly, Nate and I managed to keep every interaction entirely superficial since then. Let me tell you, that was no easy feat in our small social circles. Nate had it all but written on his forehead he wanted nothing more to do with me, so I figured too much alcohol had gotten to him. I needed to get my head out of my ass and stop wishing he wanted more.

The moment the door clicked shut behind him, I was just drunk enough to be pissed off. "What the hell are you doing here?" I demanded.

He crossed the room, stopping maybe a foot away from me.

"What the hell are *you* doing here?" he countered in return, his eyes narrowing and his words coming out sharp.

"What does it look like I'm doing? I'm doing this fundraiser for the hospital. Get the hell out of here." I waved my hand. "Someone just paid five thousand bucks for a date with me, and I'm not gonna screw it up by having you here when they show up," I muttered, my speech slurring a little.

Nate stared at me for a beat, his eyes taking on a wicked gleam before his mouth kicked up at the corner. "Oh, you don't need to worry about that. I'm the one who bought a date with you."

My body was on fire, heat flashing through it in a rush and my belly spinning in flips at the raw desire in his eyes. Nate drove me crazy. He'd been Alex's best friend for as long as I could remember. If you'd told me I'd have thought he would be sexy when I was about ten, I'd have laughed until I peed my pants.

Everything had felt normal until sometime over a year ago. As if tectonic plates shifted in the earth, I looked at Nate one day and suddenly noticed he was obscenely hand-some. Making out with him that night was the biggest mistake I'd ever made. Desire had shifted from a loose idea into something concrete, very real, and very intense.

Nate annoyed me. He always told me what to do, just like my brother. The last thing I needed to do was to be attracted to him. Unfortunately, my body wasn't getting the memo. Just now, my panties were already giving up the fight.

"Oh, I don't think so. I'll do it all over again if I have to. I'm sure you can get a refund."

Meanwhile, my nipples stood at attention and my channel clenched, vividly remembering the feel of his fingers buried inside me.

NATE

Holly Blake stood defiantly before me, testing every ounce of my restraint. But then, she'd been testing my restraint for *years*. With her thick blonde hair loose around her shoulders and her curvy body poured into her outfit, I could hardly think.

At the moment, I couldn't even remember how I ended

up at this fucking fundraiser. Not that I had anything against fundraisers. My memory shifted into gear, kicking through the haze of raw lust Holly's mere presence had created. My buddy had roped me into going because he'd been dragged into helping out. I was there for moral support only. The last thing I expected was to bid on a date with someone. But the second I'd seen Holly on the stage, there was no fucking way I was letting someone else win a date with her.

I'd been speechless—not something that happened often, by the way—when Holly pranced out on the stage in the sexiest excuse for a nursing costume I'd ever seen. Sweet Jesus. If I didn't screw her right now against the wall, I deserved a fucking medal.

Her breasts were spilling out of the tight blouse, and I was pretty sure I could see her panties if she bent over even a little. I idly wondered if they were red to match her bright red high heels.

I took a deep breath, shackling the need galloping through my body. What the hell had she just said? Oh yeah.

"I got the winning bid, and I don't want a refund," I replied.

Her brown eyes widened and then narrowed. I was pretty sure she was a little drunk. Holly had never been one to hold back, but right now, she was a little freer than usual, let's just say.

"Why?" she demanded.

"Jesus, Holly. You're fucking parading out there half-naked. Trust me, I saw your options. I'm your best bet. The guy who I outbid was pushing seventy. Not that there's anything wrong with being old, but I don't think he's your type. What the hell are you doing here anyway?"

I knew I sounded pissed off. I also knew I had no right to feel that way, but it didn't change anything.

Holly spun around, flinging a hand up in the air and giving me the finger as she walked to the far side of the room. Not that the room was too large. She turned back to me, crossing her arms and setting her feet apart.

"What the hell are you doing here? Like I said before, I'm here to raise money for charity. That's why. And I sure as hell don't need you fucking everything up. I might actually get to meet somebody here. But now you're here, so I'm stuck with you."

My head was spinning as I tried to catch up to what she was implying. "What the fuck do you mean? You might meet someone?"

Holly sighed, letting her arms fall and resting a hand on her hip. Holly was all kinds of tempting. Her blonde hair was most often pulled up in a slapdash ponytail, and she was usually wearing scrubs. Even when she made zero effort to look good, she was sexy as sin. Dressed like this?

I was so screwed.

"I need another shot," she muttered, turning around and walking to a table in the corner where, lo and behold, there were a few bottles of alcohol. She proceeded to pour a shot of tequila and knock it back inside of a few seconds.

"It's not like my dating prospects are any good in Willow Brook," she mumbled as she turned back to face me. "I figured I'd raise a little money for this hospital thing and maybe I might actually meet someone. Not you. I didn't need to meet you."

For the second time tonight, I was speechless.

Fuck it.

I strode to her, reaching for her hands and tugging her against me.

"What do you think you're doing?" she murmured as her body bumped against mine.

"You don't need to meet anybody," I said flatly.

Holly's breath hissed through her teeth. When she gulped in air, her breasts pressed against my chest. It was then I realized my miscalculation. Because I couldn't be near Holly and not want her. Fiercely.

Having her this close meant there was no way for her to miss the fact that I was rock hard and ready. Her eyes narrowed again, and she jabbed her finger in my chest.

"You don't get to say whether or not I need to meet anybody. You're not my keeper, so don't fucking act like it."

"No. But I want you, and I know you want me. So, let's stop dancing around and do something about it."

Her mouth dropped open, her cheeks flushing bright pink and sending another shot of blood straight to my swollen cock.

"You don't know that I want you," she announced, with another jab of her finger against my chest. "You've been ignoring me anyway."

"You mean to tell me you forgot about that kiss last year," I murmured, sliding my palm down back of her spine to cup her bottom, palming it as I rocked into her slightly.

She rolled her eyes. "I'm not trying to tell you I forgot about it. But you couldn't run away fast enough. I'm not an idiot. I'm not just gonna be another chick you have a little fun with. I'm almost thirty, and I need something real, not you and your bullshit."

"Oh sweetheart, this isn't bullshit."

I finally gave into the need that I'd been holding a bay for too damn long. I fit my mouth over hers, growling at the snap of electricity the moment our lips collided.

That kiss we had a year ago? It was as if we picked up right where we left off. My body knew exactly what it wanted. I swept my tongue into the warm sweetness of her mouth, savoring the low moan coming from her throat and the way she flexed into me.

Just when I forgot where we were and what the hell I was doing, there was a sharp knock at the door. Holly broke away from me, stumbling back. The door swung open, and one of the guys who'd been helping with the tickets at the main door when I first got here stepped into the room.

"How we doing here?" he asked with a smile as his gaze swept over us.

We'd kissed maybe for a minute, yet Holly's lips were swollen, her skin was flushed, and my arousal was likely quite evident to anyone who paid attention.

Holly's gaze swung to the man. "Ethan, I'm so glad you're here. We have a problem."

What the fuck is she doing?

Holly approached Ethan, looping her arm through his, and then pointing to me. "He's not the right date. I grew up with him, so this won't work," she said flatly.

Ethan's lips tightened as he fought a smile, his gaze flicking to me and then back to her. "Sweetheart, it doesn't quite work that way. He paid for a date with you. Short of things like violence or safety, either you're going on a date with him, or we refund him his money. Unless he agrees to forfeit the date," he said carefully.

"Can't his money pay for somebody else?" Holly asked, undeterred.

I was trying to keep a level head, but now I was pissed. "No," I said sharply. "You don't have to go on a date with me. But I'm not paying for someone else. Before you go making up something ridiculous"—I paused, looking at Ethan—"her twin brother is my best friend. We've known each other forever. There's nothing nefarious here."

Ethan was quiet, his gaze bouncing between us. "Well, then I'm sure you two can figure this out. Holly," he said, gently uncurling her hand from his arm, "if you would like us to refund his money, please let me know. Otherwise, I'll leave you two alone for now."

As soon as the door shut behind him, I strode to her. Conveniently, she was standing beside the wall. I placed my hands on the wall beside her and pinned my gaze on hers.

"You're a coward," I said flatly.

"I'm not a coward!"

"I say you are. Plus, maybe you're not giving me enough credit."

"I'm sorry?"

"You're right. After that kiss last year, I kept my distance. Because I didn't want to be stupid. You're my best friend's sister, so there's that hurdle. I want you more than I've ever wanted anyone. I didn't know if I was ready to do anything about it. Now I am. The ball is in your court."

I held still for a moment before trailing my fingers down over her shoulder, teasing over her tight little nipple, and then over the soft curve of her hip. Stopping there took all of my restraint, but I managed it.

I stepped back. "You owe me a date. Tell me now if you're backing out. I'll leave you alone if you are, but don't play games with me."

Holly's breath came in shallow little pants. She shifted her legs, and I heard her rubbing her thighs together, just barely. I hadn't forgotten how wet she'd been last year when I lost my damn mind and almost fucked her at a party.

She stared at me, lifting her chin slightly. "I'm not backing out. When and where?"

"Your call. But not tonight. Let me make one thing clear, though. It will be a real date. You don't get to say, let's grab drinks at Wildlands, or coffee at Firehouse Café. Hell no. Dinner and a hotel. I did pay five thousand dollars, after all."

"I'm not your whore," she retorted.

I closed the distance between us again, leaning forward and catching her lips in another kiss. Kissing her was like playing with dynamite. Clinging to my control, I drew away.

"No, you are absolutely not. You want this as much as I do."

———

Coming January 2019!
Burn For You

If you love steamy, small town romance, take a visit to Diamond Creek, Alaska in my Last Frontier Lodge Series. A sexy, alpha SEAL meets his match with a brainy heroine in Take Me Home. It's FREE on all retailers! Don't miss Gage & Marley's story!

Go here to sign up for information on new releases: http://jhcroixauthor.com/subscribe/

FIND MY BOOKS

Thank you for reading Melt With You! I hope you enjoyed the story. If so, you can help other readers find my books in a variety of ways.

1) Write a review!
2) Sign up for my newsletter, so you can receive information about upcoming new releases & receive a FREE copy of one of my books: http://jhcroixauthor.com/subscribe/
3) Like and follow my Amazon Author page at
https://amazon.com/author/jhcroix
4) Follow me on Bookbub at
https://www.bookbub.com/authors/j-h-croix
5) Follow me on Twitter at https://twitter.com/JHCroix
6) Like my Facebook page at
https://www.facebook.com/jhcroix

———

Into The Fire Series
Burn For Me
Slow Burn
Burn So Bad
Hot Mess
Burn So Good
Sweet Fire
Play With Fire
Melt With You
Brit Boys Sports Romance
The Play
Big Win
Out Of Bounds
Play Me
Naughty Wish
Diamond Creek Alaska Novels
When Love Comes
Follow Love
Love Unbroken
Love Untamed
Tumble Into Love
Christmas Nights
Last Frontier Lodge Novels
Take Me Home
Love at Last
Just This Once
Falling Fast
Stay With Me
When We Fall
Hold Me Close
Crazy For You
Catamount Lion Shifters
Protected Mate
Chosen Mate
Fated Mate

ACKNOWLEDGMENTS

My readers... again and again and again. Your support means the world to me. Thank you for your emails and your messages, and for making this entire journey worthwhile.

Gracious thanks to Jenn Wood for making sure I gave Harlow & Max's story everything it needed. A bow of thanks to Terri D. for catching all the details and being so kind.

To my last line of defense - Janine, Beth P., Terri E., Heather H., & Carolyne B. - thank you for making sure I don't miss anything! Yoly Cortez continues to create stunning covers for this series.

My dogs keep it real and make sure I get my story planning time with my morning runs. To my hubs who taught me there are different kinds of love. I'm lucky enough to share this crazy journey with him.

xoxo
J.H. Croix

ABOUT THE AUTHOR

USA Today Bestselling Author J. H. Croix lives in a small town in the historical farmlands of Maine with her husband and two spoiled dogs. Croix writes steamy contemporary romance with sassy independent women and rugged alpha men who aren't afraid to show some emotion. Her love for quirky small-towns and the characters that inhabit them shines through in her writing. Take a walk on the wild side of romance with her bestselling novels!

Places you can find me:
jhcroixauthor.com
jhcroix@jhcroix.com

facebook.com/jhcroix

twitter.com/jhcroix

instagram.com/jhcroix

Printed in Great Britain
by Amazon

38125132R00148